Praise for
HOTLINE

"*Hotline* is, quite simply, a spectacular book. Few novels have captured with such quiet, precise subtlety the interplay between isolation and connection that so often dominates the life of a new immigrant. There is no false veneer of sentimentality or melancholy in Dimitri Nasrallah's vivid depiction of a Lebanese immigrant's struggle to make a fresh start in 1980s Montreal. Instead, the essential humanness of *Hotline*'s characters underpins a story about our need to bond with one another, to shed our secrets, to feel in some way, in any way, seen. Nasrallah is one of my favorite writers working today, an exceptional talent who deserves to be much more widely read."

—Omar El Akkad, author of *What Strange Paradise* and *American War*

"*Hotline* is a heartwarming story about a young single mother and her son who immigrate to Montreal from Lebanon in the 1980s. It's the interiority of the mother that really makes the novel shine. Nasrallah's protagonist is naive, hopeful, strong, curious, fearful and, oh my god, so brave. We so often ascribe masculine qualities to bravery and survival. The courage it takes to build a simple life as a single mother all alone in a new world, is revealed to be delicate and feminine and caring and sweet."

—Heather O'Neill, author of *When We Lost Our Hea* *and The Lonely Hearts Hotel*

"Nasrallah's fourth novel, it takes his work to a new level of sophistication and constitutes a significant addition to the literary chronicling of the Canadian immigrant experience." —Ian McGillis, *Montreal Gazette*

"*Hotline* intertwines hope and sorrow to create a moving story that sears the heart."
—Zeahaa Rehman, *Quill & Quire*

"I admire how Nasrallah plumbs new territory with each novel. That said, underlying themes and concerns thread through his oeuvre, such as emotional and geographic exile and 'family.'"
—Ami Sands Brodoff, *Montreal Review of Books*

"A quietly transformative story, one that takes your assumptions, twists them into a shape you didn't initially see and casts them back at you in a really lovely way."
—Alison Manley, *Miramichi Reader*

"Fiction about immigrants tends toward melancholy and tragedy. Dimitri Nasrallah's new novel delivers something different. *Hotline* suggests that immigrant literature may be able to navigate its own course between the Scylla of despair and the Charybdis of naïveté. The problems of bootstraps narratives aside, happy endings are still worth writing." —Amanda Perry, *The Walrus*

HOTLINE

Also by Dimitri Nasrallah

The Bleeds

Niko

Blackbodying

HOTLINE

Dimitri Nasrallah

Other Press
New York

First published in Canada in 2022 by Véhicule Press, Montreal

Production editor: Yvonne E. Cárdenas

Typeset in Adobe Minion

1 3 5 7 9 10 8 6 4 2

Library of Congress Cataloging-in-Publication Data
Names: Nasrallah, Dimitri, 1978- author.
Title: Hotline / Dimitri Nasrallah.
Description: New York : Other Press, 2024. | "First published in
Canada in 2022 by Véhicule Press"—Title page verso.
Identifiers: LCCN 2024000180 (print) | LCCN 2024000181 (ebook) |
ISBN 9781635424683 (paperback ; acid-free paper) |
ISBN 9781635424690 (e-book)
Subjects: LCGFT: Novels.
Classification: LCC PR9199.4.N37 H68 2024 (print) |
LCC PR9199.4.N37 (ebook) | DDC 813/.6—dc23/eng/20240117
LC record available at https://lccn.loc.gov/2024000180
LC ebook record available at https://lccn.loc.gov/2024000181

for Maha

NO EXPERIENCE NECESSARY

At five minutes to two, I check my face in the mirrored walls of the building's lobby, straighten my blazer, touch up my lipstick, and then board the elevator to the sixth floor. I've been through this process many times now. I'm always hopeful that this time will turn out differently. Inshallah! I'm already finding things to like about this building: the lobby is bright and well kept; there's a security desk to keep all the abu reihas from doing drugs in the public washrooms; even the elevator is a good size. I know myself. I grow attached to little touches like this too fast, and I begin to imagine myself anywhere and everywhere in an effort to will the world to bend my way for once. I'm a dreamer. My mother always said so.

The elevator doors open at the sixth floor, where a promising white lobby and relatively clean carpeting greet me. Someone has thought to empty out the large ashtray garbage can by the elevator so it's not the first smell to backhand you when the doors slide open. Along the wall to the right is one of those modern-looking glass doors, and stencilled across it in neon-red letters is the name NUTRI-FORT.

[3]

I step inside and announce myself to the bored receptionist. "Muna Heddad," I say. "Here for the information session. We spoke earlier."

She rolls her eyes, checks her list, and then points to a room down the hall. "Follow the signs for Information Session and wait with the others. Help yourself to the free coffee."

I hope she doesn't notice my eyebrows perk up at the mention of free coffee. I find that impressive. At the end of the hall, I step into a conference room with windows facing out over the north end of the city. There's a long, wide table with a screen on one end and a dozen other people seated around it, waiting for the session to start. I drift toward the coffee station and mechanically fill a paper cup, then find a seat along the windowed side of the room. From up here, you can see the McGill University campus, and the mansions along Docteur-Penfield and des Pins, and then Mount Royal. As I wait for the meeting to begin, I try to find my home: there it is, the tall apartment building just outside the campus gates along University Street, the only place that would rent a furnished apartment to a single mother, an immigrant with no references.

A tall, sharply dressed blonde walks into the room and claims the end of the table with the slide projector and screen.

"Bon après-midi à tout le monde," she says, "and welcome to Nutri-Fort's information session on an exciting new career opportunity, for the right person. Tell me, how many of you would say that you're happy with your lives?"

A few people around the table let out nervous chuckles.

One man begins to raise his hand but then realizes the question may be more rhetorical than anything else.

The blonde smiles as she scans the room, aware that she's thrown some people off their expectations. "My name is Lise Carbonneau. I'm the general manager of Nutri-Fort's downtown Montreal branch. We have six branches across the province now, thirty-four across the country, and there are plans to expand. All this wasn't here even two years ago. 1984, that's when this company first launched in Québec, and now it's poised to grow quickly."

The ad in the back of the *La Presse* Jobs section did not give any sense of what kind of work this company did. All it said was "Consultants Needed. Base Pay + Commission. Full-time hours Mon. to Fri. Must have strong interpersonal skills. Interview Guaranteed," so I thought to myself, *why not, what do I have to lose? I've been searching for work for almost three months now. It's already November, and I've applied to every posting for a French teacher in* La Presse, Le Devoir, *the* Gazette, *with no luck at all. I'm running out of savings.* As I listen to this woman talk, ya-neh, maybe I'm a little desperate.

"Laissez-moi vous racontez une histoire, entre amis," Lise says. "Two years ago, I wasn't happy with my life. I was working as a floor manager down the street at The Bay, in charge of makeup girls. It's glamorous. Everyone knows that makeup section as one of the legends of this city's cosmetic world. But I was unsatisfied, unfulfilled by the work. The hardest part of my job was catching old women shoplifting and lecturing them while we waited for the police to arrive. I wanted a bigger challenge. I needed to believe in a vision of the future. I wanted a larger purpose to connect me to humanity's greater desire to self-actualize. Who here knows that word? Self-actualize. What does it mean?"

Lise cocks her hands on her hips and waits for an answer. I'm captivated by how easily she controls the room. I remember being nervous as a teacher in front of a roomful of kids for the first time, but I can see that this woman has thought everything through ahead of time, including what she wants us to think. I envy her already. Seizing the opportunity to make an impression before the others, I gently raise my hand.

"You." She flutters her hand in my direction.

"I think it means ... to become a better version of yourself?"

"That's it," Lise replies, smiling directly at me. Ya rabi, her gaze practically pulls aside my makeup like the thin-threaded veil it is and looks directly into my naked soul. "To become a better version of myself." *I'm using you like a prop in my performance*, her eyes say to me. *We now share a secret.* "That's exactly what I needed in my life, and that's what Nutri-Fort provided me with its patented weight-loss formula."

At this point a few of the men in the room scoff.

"You're right to think like that," Lise adds quickly, not letting the reaction pass unnoticed. "Nothing truly exceptional ever comes from staying inside your comfort zone. Who here is uncomfortable talking about their weight? How many of you have ever attempted a diet in secret, with nothing more than a how-to book or a magazine clipping to guide you? At Nutri-Fort, we believe you shouldn't have to go through that journey alone. It doesn't work. Left to your own devices, there are too many easy exits. If you want to lose weight and keep it off, you need a plan. You need to connect with people who care, who can offer you the right tools. That's the service we offer."

One of the more overweight men at the table gets up to leave, avoiding eye contact with the others as he makes his way out the door. Once the door closes behind him, Lise presses the clicker on the table and a slide appears on the screen. It is a picture of a woman who looks like her but much heavier. Even though the woman in the picture is smiling, I think she looks sad. I can see it in her eyes, yaneh, which never lie. I wonder if this is what Lise has just seen in my eyes.

"Can you believe this was me two years ago?" she says. "On my first day of work, this was the photo that was taken for my client kit. I'm sharing this with you not because I'm proud of myself, although I am. I'm telling you because the Nutri-Fort system works. It worked for me. I lost thirty-nine pounds. It's a program I believe in. Today I'll introduce you to our products and services, as well as the job you're here for: Nutri-Fort's phone consultants, who communicate with clients and build a client base. Everyone ready?"

After two more people leave, Lise begins in earnest, using slides to keep her comments on track. Ya hayete, how has it come to this, I wonder as she discusses the company's philosophy on weight gain, how the food packets are designed to take the guesswork out of daily calorie regiments so clients can tackle the mathematical ends of obesity. All I want to do is teach, to have my own classroom and my own group of students. As she gives us some background information on how the program was first developed in California, I imagine how I would decorate its walls with famous quotes and arrange the desks for the students to sit in groups, and we would learn grammar and literature, but also songs and games. I am good with kids, a very generous teacher. It was what I did best in Beirut, during those few breaks in the war when the schools reopened.

"But the long-term success of the program resides in people like you and me," Lise says. "The personal support we can offer to all the feelings that come along with months or years or lifetimes of a body's fluctuation. The food packages are a way into the daily routines of someone's life, and once you get them on the phone and talking, the client will begin to wander sideways or backwards into the real reasons they've gained that weight. The phones are the most sensitive part of the job, and many consultants are not ready to handle the onslaught of human emotions they encounter: the secrecy, the neediness, the little lies, the passive aggression, the silences, the snaps, the attacks. People don't always call here with their best selves on offer, but with a controlled structure you can draw that optimal persona from them and they can learn to accept and even anticipate your trespass into their personal lives."

Next, Lise covers how regional advertising campaigns in magazines, newspapers and television bring in new clients through a hotline number, 1-800-MOI-FORT. "Hard to forget, hein?" Lise says. "That's the point. It sticks in your head until you're ready." When people finally muster the courage to pick up the phone, they are automatically directed to a consultant for follow-through. "Just like that, you're talking to someone who understands your problem." She discusses how sales numbers determine commission. "Those of you who are well organized will see your efforts rewarded."

Lise finishes by saying, "Don't you ever feel there are some things in the world that you just don't want to talk about with the people in your lives? What we offer is a little window to the outside, someone our clients can confide in with information that's too sensitive to reveal in their daily interactions. Many people don't have daily interactions at all. Our hotline is a shortcut through all those complications of daily life. On the phone, you may be filling in for a loved one, you may be a coach, or even a disciplinarian. People won't tell you what they need, but if you make it your skill to figure it out from what they do say, then you will be successful. I'm going to leave these information packages here. At the back, you'll find an application sheet. If you're interested, fill one out and leave it at the front desk. You can expect a call from us in the next two days. If you're selected, we start Monday."

With that, she bids us a good afternoon and leaves the conference room. Once she's safely down the hall, about half the people around the table, including all the men, gather their things and make their way out without even looking through the information package.

Some others at the table have begun complaining quietly about how this is one of those scams they hear about on TV. One woman shares the story of a friend who tried this sort of service, and it's really just about siphoning as much money as possible from these poor people looking for help.

Ya rabi I can't help but be drawn to the stack Lise has left behind. I find certain people quite magnetic. It's not a question of what they say, but who they are. Without listening to any more gossip, I walk to the front of the room and pick up an information package. Back at my seat, I fill out an application. One or two other women follow my lead. The rest take this as their cue to leave and continue with their search for better opportunities. Ya hayete, I don't really have a choice now, do I?

Across from the Nutri-Fort office is Dorchester Square, where it's not safe to walk after dark, but now that I have some time after the information session, I sit on one of the dirty benches that's not been taken already by the sleeping homeless or old people feeding the pigeons. The pigeons gather around my legs too, bobbing their little heads as if to ask, *Do you have bread for us?* I don't. They soon know to leave me alone. *Will you take the job if they call you, Muna?* I ask myself.

I head up the street to Bens, a diner on the corner of Metcalfe and De Maisonneuve, and look through the free newspapers. They know me there now, and they've started to give me these looks, like I'm a hableh. I order a black coffee and half a bagel, the cheapest special on the menu, even though what passes for coffee here is actually just bitter black water, and I go through the Jobs sections of all the newspapers the restaurant provides for their customers. I underline a few numbers, get my reading glasses from my purse, fold the paper in half, and, with a pen in hand, I go to the phone booth in the back to make more inquiries. The booth is occupied. I wait my turn.

When the booth door slides open, a nervous-looking young man who smells like an ashtray steps out. With my sleeve covering my nose, I step inside and opt to keep the door open because the booth smells like a donkey's cage and, really, I don't understand how some people let themselves go. Pulling a Kleenex from my purse, I pick up the receiver, push in my quarter, which I now recognize as the biggest silver coin in my coin pouch, and dial the first number I've circled in the ad.

"Ahem, oui, bonjour. I'm calling about your ad in *La Presse* for …" and I scan the ad quickly to find the term they used. I ask a few questions about the job and the person on the other line gives me quick, curt responses or avoids answering altogether. It's not looking too good. Ya-neh, I'm used to this.

Freeing up the phone booth for the next caller, I return to my stool at the counter, where my cold, bitter coffee awaits. My accent, I've become convinced, has been an obstacle in every single attempt to find work, even though I speak French fluently and have a few years' experience teaching it at the grade-school level. I sit down in front of the pile of newspapers and continue scanning the ads, but my heart's not in it anymore for the day.

With nothing else to do until I have to pick up Omar from school, I spend the rest of the day walking around the city aimlessly. I don't want to go back to the apartment and just sit there, worrying about how I only have enough savings left for the next month. I walk back and forth along rue Sainte-Catherine. I know the area well enough by now, at least as far as boulevard Saint-Laurent, soon after Complexe Desjardins. Yaneh east of there, the city really changes and there are strip clubs and abu reiha hotels, with the prostitutes and drug users hanging around the shop fronts all day and night, and being new in this country, I don't want any trouble. In the other direction, I usually walk as far as the Montreal Forum. After Atwater, the street enters Westmount and suddenly everything looks brighter and wealthier. Too far past Complexe Alexis Nihon and I begin to feel like a maid walking past all the rich wives in fine jewelry and Mercedes Benzes, smoking Yves Saint-Laurent menthol lights.

In the few months living here, I've walked back and forth along this stretch of Sainte-Catherine between Saint-Laurent and Atwater many times, chasing job interviews, to take the metro, to shop at The Bay or Eaton's or Simpsons. I like exploring the underground parts of the city and all the new shops. Ya Allah, it's so modern down there with its bright lights and striking tile patterns, like walking in a space station. Along the downtown streets, you can still see how many of Montreal's buildings are a hundred years old. But down in the underground city connecting the metro stations, everything is brand new and there are lush vines and manicured ponds and flowing escalators and public benches where anyone can sit, pastel trash cans at every turn, and you can't walk five minutes without passing a fast-food restaurant or a dry cleaner or an old man in a tiny booth who'll replace your watch's battery. I can walk into Complexe Desjardins, the most modern of the underground shopping malls I've found so far, and find myself traveling through a winding network of marble corridors across the downtown before I come back up to street level around Place Bonaventure.

I explore like this, in large circles with no plan in mind other than to pass the time, until finally it's a quarter past three and I'm standing in front of Omar's school. I wait for him to find me among all the parents at the chain-link fence that separates the sidewalk from the schoolyard. The afternoon has turned cold and the breeze has begun to bite at my ears. Finally I see him and he sees me, and even though this happens every weekday, I let out a sigh of relief. Ever since arriving in this country, I feel anxious all the time about the littlest things.

"Mama!" he calls out, running to me.

"Keefak, ya ibneh?" I say, rubbing his hair. "Good day at school?"

He shrugs and we begin to walk up the street to our apartment. He usually doesn't say much right after school and I don't press too hard, even though I want to know everything.

We live on the fifth floor in a one-bedroom furnished apartment. I've given Omar the bedroom because an eight-year-old boy should still be able to keep his toys all over the floor and be properly rested for school. I keep the ironing board and our laundry in there too, and some boxes and other things I'm slowly collecting for the day we move out of here. In the main room, there's our living room and dining table and kitchen all in one – a kitchenette they call it here, smallah. There's the table where we eat all our meals on one end, and where I keep all my job application papers on the other. Weighing down the papers is a small wooden horse that was carved from the broken leg of my marriage bed. It was a toy for Omar once, carved by his father. But Omar was too young at the time, and he no longer remembers where it came from. Now I use it as a table decoration, the only item in this small apartment that distinguishes us from everyone else who ever lived here.

A few feet away, there's the sofa where Omar watches a small TV from the 1970s. It's not our TV, but that doesn't matter to Omar as long as the rabbit ears are well-positioned and we get minimal squiggles for his favorite show. I let him watch as much TV as he wants because it's like practice. He's in a classe d'acceuil, where they put all the children who don't know enough French yet. If not the TV, who else is going to talk to him that much? He's getting better at mimicking its inflections.

I bring Omar a snack and settle down beside him. His first choice on Thursday nights is *ALF*, an American show dubbed in French, on CFTM 10. It involves this giant puppet who is supposed be an alien. His name is Alf – it means *a thousand* in Arabic. This Alf lives with a family in their home. He can't leave the house, and it turns out they must keep him in secret. But the family, especially those parents, seems unsure about what they'll do: can they tolerate this alien living with them forever, or should they kick him out? Meanwhile, he keeps complicating their lives. As Omar laughs and points at the screen – because it's funny but in a stupid way; yaneh they're all idiots – all I can do is smile and stroke his hair, this adorable little boy, and check for lice now and then as the notice he received from school has directed me to do. I can't tell him that his own mama is an Alf too, that Alf isn't a joke but a serious tragedy. I can't tell him I'll have to take any job that comes my way now so he can at least keep watching his favorite show until the season finale, which the commercials inform us is coming up on December 18.

After the show ends, there's a five-minute newsbreak, a weather report, a preview of tonight's lottery.

"Yallah, ya habibi," I say, pulling him off the sofa. "Time to go brush your teeth."

"Do I have to go to school tomorrow?" he asks.

"One more day and then it's the weekend. Inshallah it will be nice out and we'll go for a walk."

I take Omar by the hand and walk him over to the tiny bathroom, where I have to stand outside as he brushes his teeth because there isn't enough room for both of us unless I stand in the shower stall. Once he's done, we head into his room where he changes into his pajamas as I pick toys up off the floor and place them in a bin.

"Yaneh, do you want me to break my foot on one of these?" I complain.

"La, Mama," he says, but he's not really paying me much attention by then, as he's tired and already crawling under the covers. Out of nowhere, he begins to whimper.

"What's wrong, my sweet?" I ask, turning out the light and crawling into the bed beside him. "Tell Mama."

We lie in a shaft of light streaming in from the hall and look at each other without saying anything. He appears flustered, as if trying to decide on the words to use, and then simply spits out, "I'm sad."

I cuddle in closer so that my face is right next to his,

and with the blanket covering us, I whisper, "Did something happen at school?"

He shrugs. With Omar, I always have to dig for the smallest answers.

"Is it your teacher?"

He shakes his head.

"Is it the other kids? Did someone say something?"

"Some boys wouldn't let me play with them. But I didn't understand what they were saying, so I kept playing. Then they pushed me out of the game, and all the other kids laughed."

"Who would do that?" I coo. "That's horrible."

"They would," he says, his face hot under the blanket. "They did."

"You know what I say to people who behave like that?"

"What?"

"*Kol khara!*" I exclaim, with a crazed look on my face.

He laughs. "I can't say that!"

"Of course, you have every right to tell them to eat shit," I say, stroking his hair. "No one knows what we're talking about anyway, so you go ahead and tell them how you feel, and they won't understand a thing." I kiss his forehead. "I'm kidding, habibi. I know it's hard for you. It's hard for me too. It won't last forever. It's just because we're new. Just you wait. By this time next year, we won't remember any of this."

"If you say so, Mama."

"Inshallah, my heart. Inshallah." I kiss him on the forehead and sing him a Lebanese lullaby about a carrier pigeon transporting messages of love between two young lovers trapped on different rooftops. It's a very old song that my mother sang to me and her mother sang to her, and now every night I sing it to Omar, and because I've sung it to him since before he can remember, he sings along. It's an endless song; it goes round and round, from verse to chorus to verse and back again until it lulls a child into dreams. Once he drops off, I lie there silently next to him, not wanting to move a muscle because this is the only perfect part of my day, the only part I wouldn't trade if I had half a chance. I listen to his breathing. I can tell when he's sound asleep from the way he takes in and lets out air. Ever so slowly, I raise the blanket off my chest and get out of the bed. I walk toward the light in the hall, take one look back from the doorway, and close the bedroom door behind me, leaving it ajar just so, for a little air and light to circulate through.

Back in the living room, I push aside the coffee table and pull out the sofa bed. I'd never seen a sofa bed before moving here. In Beirut, a living room is something you fuss over like a peacock's feathers and present to your larger family and friends as the fruit of all your accomplishments. But here, it's just where I have to pull away a couch's cushions at night before wrestling with the cranky metal frame of a bed that doesn't want to open up for me. Ya hayete. I can't blame it. I'm sure the furniture in this apartment has witnessed its share of broken dreams and broken hearts. They've all managed to move on; the proof of it is that I am here now. With its water-stained kitchen ceiling, its mold in the bathroom, its scuttling sounds in the middle of the night, and the paper-thin walls, it's not a place anyone would want to stay for long. I hope I am next to go, although if I don't find work in the next three weeks, it may very well be out to the street.

I pull the duvet and pillow down from the closet. They're not mine, of course. Other people have huddled in them for warmth before, and there's something of all the abu reihas that I can't get out in the wash. I spread them out, change into my pajamas, and lie down to drift away in the light of the flickering TV at low volume, in the darkened room. It's not that late, but the sun is setting earlier than usual, and it feels late. I'm tired, and this is the only time I have to myself, to wallow.

I'm so sad for him! It breaks my heart every time he tells me about some little sharmoot at school who insults him or pushes him or takes his lunch. I want for him to love and be loved by this new world, to make this city his own if only it will let him. My only solace is that being pushed around at school is an improvement from not going to school at all or worrying a car bomb will explode as we return from the grocery store. This has to be better.

Omar is still young enough for his memory to fade away. He can leave the ghost of his father behind. It's been two and a half years since that fateful March morning in 1984. Without our old apartment to look at, without Halim's empty side of the bed, Halim's seat at the kitchen table, Halim's ashtray on the bookshelf, Halim's mechanic's coveralls still hanging in the closet, Halim's grease-covered shoes at the door, without all those reminders around us, Omar can begin to forget what happened. He was not even six then. I pray my little man remembers only sketches of it by the time he grows up, and that it won't break him on the inside as it has me. Inshallah!

Friday morning, I'm rushing around the apartment to get Omar ready so he won't be late to school again, and the phone rings. My heart jumps. The phone never rings.

"Bonjour, Madame Muna Heddad?"

"Oui, that's me."

"This is Christine from Nutri-Fort. You filled out an application earlier this week for one of our phone-consulting opportunities?"

"That's right."

"We'd like you to come in Monday for a paid training session. Are you still available?"

"Yes, I am."

"Perfect. We'll see you at nine. Have a great weekend!"

"You too."

I hang up and sit down at the table where Omar's eating a bowl of Froot Loops.

"Who was that?" he asks.

"Work. Mama got a job, habibi."

"Yay!" He raises both of his hands up in the air like someone has scored a goal in a soccer match, and I can't help but laugh at his enthusiasm. I'm glad at least one of us feels that way.

"Yay!" I say, raising my hands to cheer too. We both cheer together. "Yallah, finish up and put on your shoes. We have to go."

Omar brushes his teeth, slips on his shoes and buttons his jacket. I'm relieved to finally have a job offer. We won't go homeless next month. But I'm landing very far away from where I wanted to land. I am a teacher, not a diet coach. I'm not exactly enamored by the prospect of listening to rich housewives complain about their weight. Yaneh, it's just good to have some room to breathe. I gather my purse, my briefcase of résumés, and my coat. I'll keep applying and see what happens.

We walk around the corner, and I drop Omar off at his school. It suddenly occurs to me as I wave goodbye that next week he'll need a key for the apartment. I'll have to trust him to walk home without me. Can I do that? If I don't get back from work until five thirty, then he will have to be home alone for two hours. If he makes it safely. This morning is very cold, I note as a freezing wind cuts across his schoolyard. I imagine my habibi trudging along on a street he doesn't recognize, lost and underdressed, completely unprepared for what I've asked him to do.

One of the many reasons I want to be a teacher is that I'll finish my day at the same time as Omar. That's why the first thing I did after we arrived is apply to the Catholic school board, which is the French school system here, and the Protestant school board, which is more English. Over the last few months, I've applied to private schools, tutoring centers. I even went to visit individual schools without an appointment, to see if I could corner an overworked principal in need of a teacher. I worked furiously to get applications in on time, I photocopied the French-version résumé I'd brought with me from Lebanon, hand-delivering it to schools and school boards alike, and no one gave me even a second glance. All the secretaries greeted me with thin smiles. *No, the principal isn't available at the moment. No, we don't call candidates back until we've reviewed all the submissions.* I've never gotten a call back from a French school or even an English-language school where French is taught as a special subject. Just a form letter thanking me for my application.

Last month, I finally received an interview with a frazzled English woman at a French-tutoring service run out of a basement-level office in the underground city around Peel metro. She seemed busy with her work even as she asked me questions. I told her about my approach to grammar, the lesson plans I typically employ. I told her about my rapport with past students, my ability to work with different age groups. The longer I spoke, the more aware I became of her attention to my lips. At least in the end, she was honest with me and said what I was sure everyone else around me was already thinking.

"Listen, lady, I'm sure you're very good at what you do, but you can't work here."

"I'm sorry. Is there no opening?"

"No, there is, but I can't hire you. And to be honest, no one else will either."

"What am I doing wrong?"

"No, you speak very well. It's just that, we're in Qué-bec. I see you're new and so maybe you don't know, but there are so many French teachers I can hire who are al-ready from here. Why would I hire a foreigner to teach other foreigners? Would you? Do you see what I mean? The people who are my clients, they want a way in, by learning French from someone who can teach them how to talk to people here."

"But it's just a language. My ability to teach should count for something."

"About that." The woman looked at my résumé. "So let me get this right. You've never taught in Canada. You don't have a teaching degree from Canada or a TEFL certificate. Those are two very important things. You're not qualified, my dear."

I sat back in her office. I was utterly dejected. She thought so poorly of me that she'd had to tell me directly to my face that I was going the wrong way. I was embar-rassed to be there, in the basement of that shopping cen-ter. "It's sad," I confessed. "I was told before I moved here that being a French teacher would be an asset. That I could do well here. It's why I came and moved my life."

"What can I tell you? It is an asset, to get into the country. But not to compete for these jobs."

"What am I supposed to do?"

"I feel for you, I really do. It's not me. I'm just telling you how things work. This is a French province. Definitely your French will help you in everyday life – and really, you speak it so well, I love your accent, so Old World – but it's not who people want to teach the language here. They've got a particular kind of French. They're very specific about how it sounds. We're not in Paris or," she ran her eyes down the résumé, "… Beirut."

"I don't know what else I can do," I said, more to myself than to her.

"I'll tell you what I tell all the other immigrants who come in here looking for work. Move to Toronto. They need French teachers in all their schools, and their French sucks. None of the *pure laines* wants to live down the 401. They hate that province, and so you've got yourself an opening. I just want to tell you how things are, so you don't waste any more of your time. That, or maybe go back to school. You're still very young. You could get a teaching diploma in just a few years."

I thanked her for her time; after all I had evidently wasted so much of it. I rode the escalator back outside to de Maisonneuve Boulevard, and that's when I told her to kol khara!

But a month later I feel like I'm about to give up. Ya rabi, today feels like my last chance to prove her wrong. So after I drop Omar off at school, I walk back down to Ben's, take my seat at one of the spinning chrome bar-stools along the counter, place my order for a coffee and half a bagel, and begin searching through the Jobs section of the first available newspaper.

There's an old movie on Radio-Canada, the kind I remember my father taking me to see at our neighborhood movie theater back in the 1960s, when I was a little girl around Omar's age. This one stars Louis de Funès. I don't really care for this old-fashioned slapstick comedy, but that doesn't matter when I have the volume down this low. The background of the French Riviera reminds me of the Corniche in Beirut, and de Funès reminds me of my father's laugh. I'm buried under the duvet of my sofa bed, and the temperature has dropped below freezing for the first time. The images dancing in front of my eyes remind me of those days. Yaneh, they're all very far away.

I am more than ten years younger than my nearest sibling. I grew up alone, my imagination my only friend. My mother was too tired to be strict and my father too old to care anymore. They let me dream, confident I would one day work out about as well or as poorly as my sister and two brothers who came before me. I was only nineteen years old when I married Halim. Ya Allah, it all seems so far away now, the life of a stranger.

Halim and I were both the youngest in our families. We met one year before the war started, in 1974, in our ancestral village of Kfar Mechki, in the mountains high above Lebanon. I was up there to spend the summer with my grandmother. He was up there working at one of his uncle's garages. He introduced himself one day at the Café Younes, the only café in the village, where I would read sometimes in the company of other bored students. He borrowed a car and drove us through the olive groves to hidden mountain streams where we splashed in the water and sunbathed on the rocks. We spent all our afternoons walking around the empty streets of Kfar Mechki in the shade of ancient buildings, while everyone else slept. He told me he loved me under the awning of Café Younes. So I fell in love. I was only seventeen then, and it was the easiest thing to do. Up in the mountains, there was no one else in the world but us.

I found out later that, even though he was a mechanic, he came from a richer family than mine. Ya rabi, I remember how we were sitting at Café Younes one evening when he admitted his parents were already planning to marry him off to a girl from another wealthy family. "I can't marry her," he told me. "We've only met twice. I feel nothing for her."

"Of course you'll marry her," I said, turning cold to him. "You can't say no to your father."

"I want you," he said, taking my face in his hands.

"You're going to break my heart," I said. "I can see it in your eyes."

But when that summer ended, we drove back down to Beirut and Halim actually backed out of the arrangement, to the great embarrassment of his family. Soon after, he told them he was in love with me.

I come from a family that's never had it simple. My grandmother once told me that, centuries ago, my ancestors left Kfar Mechki for Palestine, where they tended a grove of olive trees that sustained them for almost two hundred years. But thirty-eight years ago, all my family, my parents and grandparents, aunts and uncles, were forced to walk back up from Palestine with all the belongings they could carry. In Lebanon, we had nothing; we are like refugees with old, tenuous roots to a land where someone forgot to rip us out. Yaneh, even though I was born there, and our ancestors lived in Lebanon's mountains hundreds of years ago, in no one's mind could I ever belong to Lebanon again.

Because of that, and since I was blamed for the arranged marriage falling apart, Halim's father didn't want our marriage to happen. It was left to my father, ever the enterprising Palestinian at heart, to pursue a series of negotiations held throughout dinners and other weddings over the next two years. Many generations ago, he implored them, our two families had been friends. This is the kind of argument you have to make with a Khoury, nothing less than a destiny restored, a duty to a much longer timeline.

But in the middle of all this, in 1975, the situation in the city spiraled out of everyone's control. The militias began attacking each other every day, at any and all times, and people we knew were getting into trouble and even dying just for taking the wrong road or being from the wrong group. The movie theater my father and I used to go to was bombed, just one night after we'd gone to see a movie there. After that my father sat with me in the kitchen as Mama hovered behind him at the sink wringing dish-cloths and biting her tongue, and he said, "Let's settle this before things get worse." He borrowed money and paid Halim's father what he wanted to accept our marriage. The war gave me with one hand what it took away with the other.

The night before I married, Mama came to my childhood bedroom, where I was spending my very last night alone, and said that with all this fighting, people need to hold on to something for balance, somewhere to set their feet down, breathe deeply, look around. "Marriage can do that. We entwine by nature, as all vines do." She said, "Love is an obligation that you fall in love with over time. You will get to a place where you no longer see your lives as separate. Love is a plant that grows, and you are its custodians. You do not feel it so much as care for it, explore it, be tender to its tendencies, respect it."

I remember standing apprehensively next to Halim at the altar of a Byzantine church in Kfar Mechki with all the Heddads and Khourys on a very hot Sunday in July of 1976, my much older sisters at my side, our families standing behind us, sweating, witnessing, expectant. A priest intoned prayers and psalms, then brought Halim's and my hands together. We exchanged rings, and we kissed to complete the union. Applause followed, jubilant with relief on my side, unhurried with disappointment on his.

And nineteen months later, I gave birth to Omar. He was born in the bedroom off my grandmother's kitchen, in the same room that had been mine during all my summers spent in the mountains. He was born at dawn, in the bed

I shared with Halim ever since we began staying in Kfar Mechki to escape the battles raging in Beirut. Whenever the fighting in the city would get too close, we would drive up there in our beat-up BMW hatchback together. Ya hayete, the labor lasted three days. I remember the light outside the window rising, moving, and falling across hours, the rustling of cedar branches in the wind between contractions, a damp cloth that dripped down my forehead and into my eyes. I felt as if a claw had scraped me clean. I had not intended to get pregnant. It was hard enough finishing my studies with all this fighting. This was not a time for children. But children are a gift no matter when they arrive.

Omar was quiet; he barely cried. He had this shock of black hair and the eyebrows of an old man. He wouldn't take my nipple right away. We worried for his health. He was underweight. We couldn't go back down to the city to see if our apartment had been spared. We wouldn't have electricity. My plants were dead. I was twenty years old, a new wife, suddenly a mother. I worried about everything. Omar was in my arms, and I loved him more than anything.

Who in Montreal cares about the war or these politics in Lebanon? What does anyone here care about the differences between Maronites and Orthodox, Copts and Druze, Sunnis and Shia; Armenians, Syrians, Palestinians, and Israelis; colonialists and communists? In this city, no one has ever had to walk home along Sherbrooke the day after the passengers of the STM's 24 bus had been slaughtered with machine guns. When was the last time a car bomb exploded outside the McGill University gates? A militia would never attack the Imperial movie theater. It's unthinkable. Montreal is prosperous enough to build a new city of neon and tile right underneath the old one. People here worry instead about things like losing weight.

In Beirut, we lived in an old apartment in Ashrafieh near the university where I was studying to become a teacher. We used to keep a transistor radio on the windowsill to find out if it was safe to go outside. I would listen to it every morning as I fed Omar in his high chair. Evenings, Halim and I listened to what the city was trying to tell us, as car horns gave way to sirens, and music to gunfire. Omar, just learning to crawl, played clueless on the floor. Outside, there was garbage everywhere. No one cared about the filth we lived in anymore. I walked to the school where I taught, books clutched against my chest, through winding paths between the growing mountains of trash. That was when I first learned that nothing we do ever disappears; like garbage it just takes on a different shape and it changes us. At the grocer's, there was little food on the shelves. Mornings were the quietest time of day. We would come up from the storage lockers where we'd spend our nights, sit at the kitchen table, and conspire about what to do as Omar napped.

"I'm so afraid," I confessed to Halim one evening, my head in my hands. "I just want to go to my classroom, visit my family, and take Omar to the doctor. How much longer can we live like this?"

Halim would pull me in with his grease-stained hand. Mama had been right. The years of war pushed us closer together. We had Omar and something to fear together.

It was not hard to see that we were stronger and safer together. We could back into each other for protection. As the war grew and our lives shrank, I learned to depend on him. Being a mechanic, he could fix almost anything in our building, even the old plumbing in the cellars that leaked over our makeshift bed. He never once took his mother's side when she berated him for living in Ashrafieh. We could have lived farther east, surrounded by the safety of his large family, but then how would I get to the university every day? No matter how much blame she poured down on me, Halim refused to pay her any attention. He loved Omar and me, but he loved to spite her too.

"Now I'm a teacher but there are no schools anymore," I said one night after I finally graduated. "Your mother is right about me."

"I will never admit that my mother is right," he said to comfort me. I laughed, but I knew at least a little part of it was true.

I remember the day my niece was killed by a car bomb not far from our building. I held my older sister as she wept on the floor. "I don't want this for Omar," I said to Halim that evening. I pulled my child closer, cradled him, afraid to be alone in my own skin. "I can't bear the thought."

That's when we first began to say out loud what we were both thinking. Where can we go, what can we do there, what would we take? In 1982, the Israelis got involved and attacked Beirut, and so we went to Cyprus. Halim spent hours at a call center there, making long-distance arrangements with the French embassy through one of his brothers who lived in Marseilles.

He told me, "I found out that you being a French teacher, it can help us if we travel. Yaneh, all your education can help us. I've been talking to an agency that helps people immigrate. There is a place in Canada that will move us ahead in line because your job and degree are proof that you know the language well enough to work there."

"That's so far away," I said. We were strolling along the boardwalk, pushing Omar in the stroller we rarely got to use anymore in Lebanon. In Cyprus, we could go for a walk in the evening. "We'll never see anyone ever again."

"It's a new start. We can't live our whole lives like this, no electricity, garbage everywhere, my family adding pressure, having to make plans if we want to travel more than a few streets, sleeping underground every night. We don't have much time left to do something with our lives. What do we accomplish if we stay here? At best, we become survivors."

That summer I turned twenty-four and Halim completed the immigration papers from Cyprus, where a man in an otherwise empty office filed the many documents into a fax machine as we looked on, page after page I hadn't even bothered to read, and then handed us a receipt stating that they had arrived at the French immigration agency. We paid him a lot of money, all in American dollars we'd spent half a day securing from a bank. The process takes years, we were told. Don't expect anything too soon. We returned to Beirut and went on with our lives. We packed in preparation: four suitcases and a collection of important papers ready at any time beside the storage-room bed.

That's how we lived until that fateful morning in March of 1984. By then, the Lebanese Army's control of our streets had collapsed and everything was more chaotic than ever. As the militias fought for the neighborhood's boundaries again, some apartments in our building were looted. We cowered in the cellar with a few other neighbors who hadn't driven off to the mountains or who had grown too brazen or too old to care anymore if they lived or died. As neighbors brewed coffee on propane-gas canisters, I would rock Omar – who was a young boy by then – back and forth to get him to fall asleep.

One morning, after a night of intense shelling, Halim and I came up the stairs to find that outside our building's door a cloud of gray dust was floating eerily in the silence.

"Should we stay or should we go?" Halim asked.

"We can't stay," I said. "I can't make it through another night. I'm so afraid."

"I don't think the streets are safe yet," he said.

I was trembling, paralyzed with fear. "Ya Allah, I'm suffocating. I feel like I'm going to die."

He pulled me in and held me. "We should drive up into the mountains as soon as we can."

Halim stared out from the doorway for a long time, planning his next move. How could we get to Kfar Mechki, how could we find our way back to that place above the clouds where we first began? He would have to walk around the corner to enter the underground lot where we kept the car. Not a person stirred in the fog of smoke and dust.

"Be ready to go when I pull up," he said, and then he went downstairs to retrieve two of our suitcases.

When he returned, he stood in the doorway, where I helped him wrap a white undershirt around his face to protect him from the dust. If only I'd known it would be the last time I ever saw those eyes, then I would have paid closer attention. Were his eyes trembling? Could I feel his breath through the shirt's gauze? Did he look at me longingly before he stepped out? I don't know. I was already running downstairs to gather Omar and whatever else I could carry. I came back up, holding our son in my arms, and waited. I waited for a long time. Halim didn't come back. Later in the afternoon, a neighbor went out and found our suitcases. They were abandoned on the sidewalk, right after the corner. He had never made it to the garage. The car was still down there, but its keys had disappeared along with Halim.

I get so lost in my memories sometimes. I haven't even noticed that the de Funès movie has ended. It's why I try to not think about Halim or Lebanon during the daytime when I need to be invested in everything that's happening around me, but at night I can't help it. As I get up to turn off the TV I see that the next program on is one of those late-night infomercials. Tayeb, I usually don't watch them, but this one is for Nutri-Fort. A trim, confident woman beams at the row of food boxes on the counter in front of her, as the hotline number flashes across the screen.

On Monday morning I arrive at the Nutri-Fort office and the receptionist finds my name on a clipboard.

"Muna Heddad? Yes, one of the new girls," she says, cocking her eyebrow at me, as if to confirm that I look guilty of allowing myself to stumble so low as this. "Come with me."

She leads me into the open office floor with rows of desks to an empty one that's to be mine. As I set down my purse, I look at the desktop and the worn chair and wonder, *how many people have sat here before me, and how long did each of them last?*

"Meeting in the conference room in half an hour," the receptionist says, pointing out one of the doors along the side of the room. "Get comfortable. See you then."

I sit down and take note of what's on my desk. There's a complicated-looking telephone with way more buttons than I can understand, a headset, and a blue binder, which I draw toward me and open. It's full, maybe a hundred pages. Each page is a profile of a different person, with their name, age, occupation, marital status, and how long they've been a client at Nutri-Fort. Then a description of the case so far. I close the binder, slide it back in its place, and open the drawer to find a notepad, a stapler, a few pens and markers. At the edge of the desk I have a nameplate. Surprised, I turn it around and see that it only says TRAINEE. I look around at the floor of desks where mostly other women sit, already taking phone calls. Yaneh, it seems easy enough, so how bad can this be until I get a better job? I have to keep a positive attitude.

Five minutes early, I head to the conference room, where I recognize only one person from the information session. But she doesn't appear to want to acknowledge me, so I sit along the other side of the table. By the time the meeting begins, there are twenty of us around the table and a few more standing along the sides of the room.

Lise Carbonneau enters pushing a cart filled with the same yellow, orange, and red boxes I saw on the infomercial over the weekend. She circles around to the front of the table and places the cart to the side of her screen so we can all see the boxes clearly. The slide on the screen reads *Welcome to Nutri-Fort* in large red letters, and then the hotline number and the tagline (*A life-changing decision!*) in smaller letters below.

"Hello, new consultants," she says. "Congratulations on being selected to represent Nutri-Fort on our province-wide phone network. I hope this is the beginning of a long journey for you here. For some of you, it may even be an opportunity for growth and careers! There's no telling just how far or how fast the nutrition-consultation industry will grow. Today, I'll be setting you up with all you need to know about our products and how to work the phones."

For the next half hour, Lise confidently presents each of the boxes on her cart, along with a slide highlighting the nutritional values of each. The trick to the system is that all the boxes break down to three different Calorie Rankings: one for breakfast (yellow), lunch (orange), and dinner (red). That makes it easier for people to know what to eat when. Even more convenient, each color series of boxes is calibrated to contain the exact same number of calories; all breakfasts are two hundred calories, lunches four hundred calories, and dinners six hundred calories. The Nutri-Fort system eliminates the guesswork of eating by organizing your meals and calorie intake for you. "And you can mix and match along the way," Lise says, "which is so much fun for the client."

There's the Nutri-Cheerios packaged to meet their calorie intake with 250 milliliters of skim milk, the Morning Danish, the Chicken Salad, the Garden Salad, the Pesto Pasta, the Cheese Pizza, the Chocolate Cake, and dozens of other products for sale. Some are frozen, some require refrigeration, while others can sit on the pantry shelf for weeks. Our job will be to communicate with clients who call the hotline after finding Nutri-Fort ads in magazines and newspapers. They pick up the food at Nutri-Fort stands at their nearest mall. "There's one in Complexe Guy-Favreau!" Lise beams. She guides us through how to assemble a menu for each client and demonstrates how to work the phone for a sample conversation. "Talk to them. Get a sense of their individual needs. The sooner you can make it personal, the longer their relationship with us will last."

Pulling a TV cart out from the corner of the room, Lise produces a book-sized black box, which she pushes into a machine under the screen and then presses a button. One after the next, customers who've succeeded at losing weight this way appear on the screen, testifying to what the program has done for them and how they hope it can help others. I've never seen a video before. Yaneh, it's captivating. It really gives the impression that the customers believe in the food.

Lise ends the meeting by supplying us each with a thick catalog of all the Nutri-Fort products. "It doesn't matter where you come from," she says, "this is your bible now." There's a smattering of laugher across the room. Lise joins in and then says, "So go back to your desks and spend the rest of the day getting to know this guide inside and out. Come up with combinations, menu ideas, go to the storeroom and take some of the samples home to test out their taste. The more you know the product, the better."

The heavy catalog in my arms, I return to my desk and spend the rest of the morning leafing through its pages. Each meal comes with a photo, an ingredients list, a flavor profile, a nutritional chart, and some suggested pairings. I pull the notepad from the desk drawer and write down meal names as I read because it helps me remember them.

That evening, I leave with some of the boxes from the storeroom that look most promising, to taste them for myself and also because shopping is expensive and I won't be paid for another two weeks. It's getting cold out now, and the sun is already setting. My jacket feels too thin, and I worry that I sent Omar to school underdressed. I hurry up University Street, eager to get back to our apartment as fast as possible. Over the weekend, when I went to speak to the building manager, Mr. Saltzman, about getting another copy of the key, I asked if he knew anyone who could watch Omar for two hours after school. He said he'd make sure the boy got into the building okay. "I'm a grandfather myself fourteen times over," he said, as if to assure me that he wasn't a sharmoot and I didn't have to worry. But I always worry a little, and it's the first time Omar has been alone for this long.

When I get to the building, Mr. Saltzman is there in his glass-walled office, and he must see the concern in my eyes all the way from his desk as I search my purse for my keys because he buzzes me in. "He's A-okay," he says once I'm in, looking back at his little TV screen. "Buzzed him in at around half past three."

"Thank you, Mr. Saltzman, it's a real help," I say, pressing the elevator button.

He waves it off. "Have a good evening, Ms. Heddad."

Before the elevator doors open, I walk back to his door. "Can I ask you one more question?"

He looks up and adjusts his thick glasses.

"Where can I get some winter coats … on a budget?"

"Well, if you want a deal, you go to the eighth floor of the Eaton's. But if you need something to get by for cheap," he ventures, "check the Vêtements 2000."

"Okay. I know about Eaton's. Where is this Vêtements 2000?"

He writes me down an address.

"Shukran, Mr. Saltzman. I mean, thank you. Sorry, I'm tired."

"It's open till eight."

I head up to the fifth floor and unlock the apartment door to find Omar parked on the couch watching a game show with a bowl of cereal in his lap.

"Hi, Mama," I say, using an old Lebanese endearment of calling him what he calls me as I set down my bags and kiss his forehead. "Good day?"

"Uh-huh," he mumbles, not really looking up.

"Were you cold? I was cold."

He nods.

"I think it's going to snow soon, habibi." I walk over to the window and look out at the gusting darkness outside. "Want to go buy a jacket?"

"I'm tired," he says, stretching.

"Me too," I say. I sit down next to him on the couch and pick a Froot Loop from his bowl. "But there's no other time to do it. I think it's going to snow, and I don't want us to get caught with nothing. I don't want you to get sick. If you come with me, I'll make you a hamburger after."

"Okay," he says.

I kiss the top of his head and pull him off the couch. "Yallah, let's go now so we can get back already."

Outside, the sky has turned black. We walk down University Street, through crowds of students leaving the McGill campus and business people finishing up late for the day. The address Mr. Saltzman has given me is along Ontario Street, farther east than I've ever walked. I've been avoiding the city's east end and hadn't thought ahead about venturing there after dark, but now that we're on our way I don't want to give up in front of Omar. Between the tall downtown buildings, the wind cuts right through our jackets.

Along the way, Omar complains that his ears are freezing, his legs tired. It's a different Montreal over here at night, and I worry that this might be a mistake, because there's no one walking on the sidewalks and the shabby little shops are giving way to row houses. I pull the collar of my flimsy trench coat up as high as it will go. By the time we arrive at the rusting doors of the Vêtements 2000, it's clear we have no choice but to find something for the walk home.

Thankfully, the fluorescent-lit store has racks of clothing as far as I can see. Tayeb, it's not as opulent as the ground floor of The Bay, where Lise Carbonneau once worked, but girls like me can't be as picky: it has the features of a regular department store, but it looks as if it's been put together from leftovers of other shopping centers.

"They have toys!" Omar comes to life again.

"Go look," I say, "but don't touch anything. I'll be over there, with the coats."

The kids section has mounds of winter wear divided in large carts with prices hanging down above them: boots ($5), snow pants ($5), coats ($5), gloves ($2), scarves ($1). Each sign has another note underneath: Full set $15. One-piece snowsuit $25.

I gather a pile and then call out, "Omar, where are you? Come try this on, habibi."

He runs over with a toy car in each hand. "Can we buy these?"

I look at the scratched-up cars he's holding up in his palms. "Min shoof. But first, see if these fit."

In the aisle, as Muzak plays in the background, I wrestle Omar into plastic snow pants and winter boots, which he's never worn before.

"They feel weird," he complains.

"Yaneh, it'll feel better when it's freezing out. Try on the coat too."

I stand back to see my handiwork: he looks like the Michelin Man. "Walk around the aisle in it. Are your toes touching the end of the shoe?"

"I'm sweating," he says.

"That's fine. Take them off. They fit, that's all Mama wanted to see. Bring those cars and let's go play in Mama's aisle. I need a coat too."

In the women's aisle, I'm not as fortunate. As Omar plays with his cars on the linoleum, I frown my way through a pile of pink and purple puffy coats, the highlights of two decades' worth of past fashions, flattened and sagging with time. I try on coats that are too large or too small, too thin or too impractical. These coats have all been stretched by the constant pulling of other people's children. I can feel the tiredness of past mothers in each garment.

Finally, I come across something that will do: a paisley three-quarter length wool coat with lining intact and a high fake-fur collar that will protect my ears and chin. I walk over to the mirrors and inspect it further: *hmmm!* A leather belt that makes it look less like a bag, pockets large enough to conceal any number of children's toys and tissues. It might even look stylish enough for the office. It's a little more expensive than some others. The Muzak cuts for a moment and a voice reminds shoppers the store will close in fifteen minutes.

"I wonder if someone died for this to end up here," I ask the mirror.

The thought of another person dying so I can be warm saddens me. Ya hayete, I'm overwhelmed with things to do, and it's enough to say I have an affinity for this article of clothing and leave it at that. Its ghost feels a little more like me than the ghosts in the other coats. The process of making it mine has begun.

We're the last ones at the cash register. Once we get back outside, it's nighttime and the wind is howling and, for the first time today, I realize that even though the world has begun to look and feel familiar in its daylight, at this unforgiving and late hour, we're still very much in a country that's not our own.

I'm so tired after my first week! It's not the job itself, but how I have to use my time around it. Yaneh, I never once thought that in coming to Montreal I would have to leave Omar alone for so long every day. In the hours I do see him, our interactions are limited to a tight schedule that involves me pushing him around from one activity to the next. Every weekday morning, I wake him up, get him washed and dressed, feed him. I walk him over to his school, and then think about him while listening to strangers on the phone at work, and when I return to the apartment, I find him on the couch, lost to a TV show, all alone. I get him up and wash his face with a warm washcloth – there, that's how you wash away the day when you come home; you start fresh – I lay out his home clothes on the bed, I prepare him a snack that's not Froot Loops (a sandwich maybe, a glass of orange juice) and when it's over we watch TV, some old game show that's on at seven o'clock every evening with a mastoul as a host, after which I start making dinner. We eat supper, the TV still on, and as I clean up I help him with his homework. I read him a story and we turn out the light. We tell each other secrets in the dark, and I kiss him goodnight. I get up as quietly as possible and make my way to the other room, where I clear the table. In my bathrobe, I watch television in the dark. At eleven, I move the coffee table, pull out the sofa bed, and check on Omar one last time after brushing my teeth and turning out the lights.

At the weight-loss center, I've settled into a routine. I just have to be organized and pragmatic, and most of the customers I've encountered so far genuinely believe those boxes are a miracle cure. My job is to talk on the phone as the food samples sit on my desk, awaiting homes: the hamburger, the ravioli, the chicken pot pie, the rice and vegetable mix, the breakfast cereal, the sandwich bars, the pizza. I am trying them all, but I find they are dry and flavorless. Yaneh, it's hard not to cheat by adding ketchup or mayonnaise or some pickled vegetables to make them taste a little better. But it's helped me make a few recommendations. The customers seem eager for guidance, and the more I give them, the more they buy.

At least my first week is over now, I say to myself in the bathroom mirror on Friday night. I don't mind talking to myself. I'm only twenty-nine. I should be able to talk to somebody in this country other than the customers on the phone lines. I've talked both too much and not enough. I tell other people what they need or want to hear, and yet there's no one to hear me. I'm beginning to see creases around my eyes. I stretch the skin there with my fingers to see how fast it bounces back. Why not talk to myself when I am the only person who will listen? *You've lived so long in such a short period of time*, I confess to my bathroom mirror. *This is what the war has done to you. It has acceler-ated time and closed so many doors, so quickly. Now all you have to look forward to anymore, ya habibti Muna, is a long hallway of closed doors.*

I once had people of my own. After Halim disap-peared, the entire neighborhood came together to help me through: my parents, my siblings, friends and connec-tions of friends, coworkers, neighbors, even Halim's fami-ly. It doesn't take much to show you care, just an extra bag of bread at the grocer's, a phone call from an old school friend, paperwork for a bank transfer.

I was devastated after Halim was kidnapped. The world wanted to rip me in half. I was numb to its advances. I was unable to take care of Omar, and I spent most of the first month in bed, between sleep and anxiety attacks. I've never felt so broken and low in my life as I did then. And peo-ple helped me along, all without me having to utter a word or anyone acknowledging it. There were silent hands all around me, leaving a glass of water and pills by the night-stand, a coffee on the stove, prepared food in the fridge, money envelopes under the door. Their silence let me keep my dignity when I needed it most. I wonder if any-one would ever do that for me here.

In Canada, people confess their problems on televi-sion and the radio, or over the phone to me. Given what I have lived through, it's ironic that I must now spend my days taking confessions through a phone to be paid a commission for each call and repeat business. Back in Beirut, I had nothing left to give anyone, least of all my-self. Halim wasn't coming back; even his family thought so. There was no funeral, no goodbye. Just acceptance of the whole ordeal ending. Years passed and I was the only one who couldn't move on. I remember sitting in my in-laws' living room as they pushed me to go to Canada, over bitter coffee and untouched finger sandwiches. "Yaneh, there's nothing to do but move on, Muna," his brothers said to me. "Consider this chance to start a new life some-where else as his gift to you. We'll help you cover some expenses too." I looked around at their faces, his mother, his father, his brothers, their housekeeper lurking in the background, and I saw people who had grown tired of supporting me after two years. "You're right." I said to them. "It's what Halim would want."

And now, not six months have passed, and that time feels like a bad dream that I can't forget. Where would Halim have even fit in this new life? Not one thing in Montreal is the same as Beirut. Here I am on my own, because of him, maybe free from a life that was turning into a prison, but cast away like a bad-luck omen too. Now I must give myself to others to survive. The world has judged that I've taken enough support for one lifetime.

I sit at my desk and make phone calls from a list of names of mostly older women who have filled out a questionnaire as part of a recent magazine advertising campaign. December is the calm before the storm, Lise told us in a team meeting. She says we have to understand the mentality of people's busy lives to see the pattern of it all. In December, people have already noticed that the weight they've gained during the hustle of the fall season – back to school, Thanksgiving, Halloween, ordering in on busy weeknights – has bulged as they put on their pants or tuck in that shirt. They're looking ahead to Christmas parties, work functions, family visits, meals, meals, meals in every direction, and they begin to bargain with themselves. I can't miss all that good stuff – turkey, wine, hors d'oeuvres, baked goods, cheese. January: that's when I'll stop and lose this weight. They're making that calculation as they wear a baggier sweater or let out the seam on that skirt. They haven't called the 1-800 number yet, but they've clipped our ad out of the magazine. They want to reach out to us, but they also want us to let them enjoy December. In their minds, they've already decided: they'll be ready to go as soon as the New Year's Day dishes have been piled into the dishwasher for the last holiday load. Yaneh, my job is to be attentive when each one of them calls in and to be brave enough to ask them questions about their weight that no one dares ask them anymore.

So far, I have only one male client. His name is Louis Laflamme. Lise says male callers are rare and may prove more complicated, psychologically, in the long run.

I let the telephone ring.

"Hydro Québec, department des comptes. Monsieur Laflamme à l'appareil."

"Oui bonjour, Monsieur Laflamme. This is Mona calling from Nutri-Fort."

Never use your real name, Lise instructed us. You never know when someone will want to look you up in the phone book and make things too personal. Pick something easy to remember, nice to say. "You should be Mona," Lise declared when she looked at my name. "Everyone loves a Mona. So easy to recall, but not you."

"Um, yes, hello."

"I'm your new weight-loss consultant. You called the Nutri-Fort hotline and left this number for a call back? I just wanted to introduce myself and take a moment to get to know a little more about you."

"Ah yes, of course." I can hear him shuffling papers on the other end.

"Is this a good time? I'd be happy to call you back at a better time if you prefer."

"Mais non, this is good. I just wasn't expecting the phone to ring, that's all."

I laugh a little, to lighten the mood. He seems tense. "Well, if it's all right, I'll just ask you a few questions about yourself."

"Of course, Mona."

When speaking on the phone, I find it's most effective to use my teaching voice. It's naturally calm, reassuring, the French polished.

"It says here you're fifty-three years old?"

"Oui, madame."

"And how would you describe your living situation: single, married, divorced, children?"

"I'm single. No children. I live alone."

"How tall are you?"

"Five foot five."

"And your weight in pounds?"

"Two hundred forty-two."

"And would you say that's steady, or going up?"

"Oh, I would say that for most of the past decade, I was hovering around two twenty. Those last twenty-two showed up in the last year."

"Are those the pounds that led you to calling us?"

"They are. At first they crept up, two, ten, fifteen. I thought it would go back down. I have to admit, I was pre-occupied with other things then. Not really thinking about myself."

"Do you know why your weight started to go up when it did, Monsieur Laflamme?"

"S'il vous plaît, call me Louis. Sure I do. My mother was dying. It was a long, complicated process. And then she died. And that was it."

"I understand, Louis. I'm so sorry for your loss."

"Thank you, Mona. Can I call you that or …"

"Mona is perfect."

"My mother had cancer. She used to live with me. Or rather, I used to live with her. She used to cook everything, but after a while she couldn't anymore."

"Was she a good cook?"

"My mom? The best! I don't want to give you the impression that I've never lived alone. It's not like that. I lived alone for many years. But then my dad had the accident at work, and when he died, oh some ten years ago now, I moved back in to help out with the house and take care of all the legal stuff that comes up when someone dies, and I never left."

I'm listening to him, and my heart breaks for this man, taking care of his mother. I don't know what to say to make him know that I'm listening, but I'm not going to pry too deeply. Tayeb, I feel that the moment I become too personal or too familiar or too presumptuous with him, it breaks our trust. I know this like I know the weight of a loved one's death. And so I inch forward instead, crawl along just enough to keep him talking. "What did you eat once your mother could no longer do the cooking?"

"Well, you know … I stopped thinking about eating like something you do with a family, you know, sitting down at a table, talking, and I began thinking about it as something that needed to be done. I always thought about it too late, or I was too tired."

"Your mind is elsewhere."

"Something like that, Mona. The food is the company you keep, not just what you put in your mouth."

"The way the Nutri-Fort system works, Louis," I say, delicately dancing back to the subject of the call, "is that you don't have to feel as if you're eating alone. You plan out your meals with a consultant, a food friend, let's say. You'll receive our catalog with all the prepared meals we offer, and then you chat with a consultant about what you like to eat, and together we build you a menu."

"And would that food friend be you, Mona?"

"Yes, it would, Louis. Twice a month, we'll chat about your food, your weight, anything on your mind that can be affecting your weight. We'll set a target, and we'll work toward it, adjusting the order as needed."

"Does it work? What if I cheat?"

"It does require a certain amount of belief. You need to have some faith in yourself and your goals. And I'm here to help you stay on course."

"Okay, well why not. I have nothing to lose, eh?"

I take him through the different plans available, their features and price points, and then take down his mailing address to send him the catalog and set him up with the billing department.

Not everyone buys a plan. Some people are just browsing, while others only want to talk. Some don't even remember calling the hotline; others get emotional or even upset once they start talking. During the first week, I talk to sixty-three clients and sign up seventeen of them. I follow the formula Lise has laid out. I listen to the clients confess how they feel powerless against their weight's onslaught.

One caller describes it as a slow wave of clay that's washed over her and hardened. The more I listen to people, the more I think that's true.

Once it gets darker out, the office windows fill with ink and it's as if we're working inside a dream. This is the best time to call, Lise says. For most people, the day's important work has been put to rest and, mentally, they've already left the building. They're at their desk like you, fidgeting, procrastinating through whatever's in front of them as they watch the daylight fade. They feel sad that they didn't make it outside or feel the light on their faces for a few minutes. They're thinking ahead to home, dinner, what to make, how it will affect their weight, how it's not really about the food but the willpower, how life is tiring.

I'm trained to ask callers when they think their weight became a problem. This is when weight complaints often evolve into stories about being preoccupied with a bad marriage, a relative dying, money problems. If we get there, then the caller will usually speak to me for a long time. Never rush them, Lise says. You want them to accept your hand, expect it to be there, to come back. You want them to feel that someone, somewhere, is thinking of them when they're not around.

I find myself thinking back to what my mother said to me before I got married: love is an obligation that you fall in love with over time. It's not a feeling so much as a caring, an exploring, a tenderness, respect. Yaneh, I think it applies to individuals as much as it does to marriages.

I return to that advice while on the phone at work, every time I'm listening to strangers complain about their lives. It calms people to have someone absorb their worries and reveal, in return, a few finely crafted words, a little bow-tied box of a thought they can open and admire. The calls are showing me a part of Montreal I would have never guessed is here. When I look for work or shop for food or clothes, people see me and they speak to me in a certain way, impersonal, mildly informative, stiff, wanting to get away. Everyone's too busy pursuing lives to pay me any attention. They would rather I remain invisible. But now I'm seeing that *no one* pays any attention to anyone else, and so many people behind these desks and phones and offices are lonely. They don't like themselves even though they've done everything they're supposed to do. They work hard, get good jobs, get married, have families, but the years still weigh them down as they try to keep up with their own expectations. Now, only a diet plan can help.

"Think of a diet as a reset," Lise instructs us in meetings. "Think of changing what you eat as feeding your brain differently. You've been on this journey for some years, and somewhere along the way you took a turn that led to this complication. You need to go back and find out where that is, but in the meantime, as you do that, let us feed you. So you don't have to worry about doing it all yourself. Let us send you packaged meals so that we can reset your body, while you can focus on the hard work of resetting your mind."

While I'm on the phone, I stare at those yellow, orange, and red boxes sitting on my desk, always there, a reminder of the goal. The cereals, the nutrition bars, the fruit sauces, the juice powders. Yaneh, I wonder if *I* like *myself*. I was a child, carefree, and then the war began and everything drowned in it. You've been on this journey for some years, ma chère Muna. I hear Lise comforting me in my own head now. Somewhere along the way, you took a turn that led to this complication, ma 'tite poulette. You need to go back and find out where that is.

On Fridays, I line up for my paycheck. The commission I made adds another $56. "Not bad for a beginner," Lise says as she scans my earnings and hands over my pay. To the next person she says, "I expect improvement, *ma chérie*."

I look down at the pay stub as I walk back to my desk. It's not very much at all. I have rent. I have groceries. After that, ya hayete, at every turn there's another expense: coats, shoes, sweaters, pants, scarves, towels, bed sheets, pillows … the list is endless. To save on food, I bring home Nutri-Fort boxes; they at least make easy school lunches for Omar. The bonus gives me a little breathing room, but I'm barely scraping by. After work, I hurry down to the bank in the underground mall to deposit my check. On Fridays, the line is long, as people fill out deposit slips and withdraw cash for the weekend. I hate leaving Omar alone so late on a Friday, right before the weekend, but the bank is closed on the weekend, and I can't make it to Monday without any money. Saturday is the only time I have to go grocery shopping and do the laundry. This entire check will be gone by next Friday.

As I walk back home from the bank, it begins to snow. I've never really seen snow before. It's breathtaking. It's just gentle flakes softly settling under the evening streetlamps.

When I get home, Mr. Saltzman, as always, gives me the thumbs-up without looking away from his TV screen, his way of saying Omar came home on time. Still, I can only breathe a sigh of relief when I finally unlock the door and see Omar sitting on the couch, lost to a TV show.

"Kifak, ya habibi." I kiss the top of his head, set down my bags, and go cook some scrambled eggs and the two hot dogs we have left in the fridge. "Yaneh sorry, we'll eat light tonight," I tell him as I bring his plate over to the TV. "Tomorrow we'll go to the supermarket."

We unfold the sofa bed and watch a movie together. Somewhere along the way, I don't know when exactly, he dozes off. I let him sleep in my bed, and I'm happy to have the warmth on such a cold night.

By Saturday morning, the sun is shining brightly again. I turn on the TV. The first weather reporter I find is on CFCF-12, one of the English stations. I can understand her about as well as I can understand Mr. Saltzman, which is to say I have to pay attention. Looking out the window as I follow along, I imagine myself inside the TV, as the weather reporter, standing in front of an aerial view of the city, and saying that the air outside is crisp and winds are light. "With fresh snow on the ground," she concludes, "we can all expect a beautiful day to kick off the weekend."

"Can we play in it?" Omar asks.

"Why not," I say, looking out the window as I have my morning coffee. He's never played in snow before, and it seems like such an affordable way to make a child happy. "We can spare some time before the supermarket."

After finishing breakfast, Omar pulls on his snow pants and waits for me at the door. Yaneh, I don't especially feel like rushing myself on my morning off, but he keeps badgering me to go, and I don't want to argue after a week of leaving him here alone all afternoon.

We walk up University Street to the mountain. It's been a few weeks since our last walk up to Mount Royal, since we can only ever really go on the weekends, and the last few have either been too rainy or too windy. The trees, which only weeks ago were covered in gold and orange, are now mostly bare, their leaves turned to a brown blanket at their feet, which is still visible in spots under the fresh snow. Omar jumps through them, crunching all he can with his new winter boots and rolling around in his new snowsuit. I'm glad we made the trip to that store because now he can enjoy something the city has to offer instead of just following me around on errands and waiting for me at home. "Look, he's laughing," I say to no one in particular as he races ahead and rolls down a hill. He's still a child, and children get depressed if they can't go outside and release some of the bad energy that builds up over time. Bad energy is like a curse. You have to shake it out of your skin, or else you get a reiha.

I'm happy to see him carefree. I'm trying to think of the last time I saw him like this, and I can't think of a moment since we moved here. As we stroll along the trail, passing other young families, dog walkers, old couples, morning hikers, and even a winter cyclist, I feel a flicker for the first time, something of that calmness I always imagined would be here, back when Halim and I planned for this move. I'm searching for that calmness as I walk along, daydreaming. Yaneh, where did I leave behind all that hope I once had?

I'm digging back through my memory. It's like a long storage closet filled with boxes, and that's how I end up back in the storage room of our building in Ashrafieh, with my head resting on Halim's shoulder as we sit on that old bed we moved down there, and – what are we doing? – we wait. That's all we ever do down there, wait for the electricity to come back or the fighting to stop, a candle glowing on the nightstand and another on a nearby shelf. It's dusty and dark, and I can hear all the neighbors chatting again, the cursing of Um Nabila, the joking of Abu Hamad. There's a backgammon game underway off in one of the corners. The storage lockers are cages, and so we're all down there like donkeys. Halim is doing what he always does down in the cellars: he's carving little wooden sculptures to pass the time, so the children can have toys. He carves dogs, cats, mice, and for Omar he's carved a horse, because even though this war has us all feeling like donkeys, on the inside we're all still horses. I remember Omar liked it so much he begged for a second one so his one horse could have a companion. But it never came to pass.

"Don't go off too far," I call to Omar – in French because we're in public – as he rolls down another hill.

"Na'im, Mama," he shouts back, oblivious and happy.

As I watch Omar walk back up the hill only to roll down again, I turn to Halim, back in the storage room. I rub his beard and feel it bristle along my palm, and I say,

"You'd like it here some days." Listening to others confess their problems has made me realize that I too have burdens I've kept locked up in cages. And so I let myself talk. He kisses the palm of my hand, and I know he agrees. I still wonder if he's really dead. Ya Allah I waited over two years. And I would still be there if not for the immigration application he was so adamant on filing with that agency when we were in Cyprus.

I still think it's my fault. We're standing in the doorway of our Ashrafieh apartment building again. It's that calm moment after a night's battle, and the cement dust hasn't settled yet. It's still spinning circles in the morning light.

"Are you sure you want me to go, Muna?" Halim asks, taking my face in his hands, peering closely into my eyes to extract my truest intentions.

I crumple into his chest. "I'm so afraid, Halim. I'll do anything to leave here. I can't take it for another night."

"Then I will go, for you."

I can see myself tying the undershirt around his face even as he says this. I've replayed this moment ten thousand times, a little differently at every turn, calibrating its cadences to inflect the pain I want to impress. He pulls me up gently by the neck and kisses me through the worn cloth. I can see the fear in his eyes. It's as if he knows what's going to happen after he turns that corner. Our eyes lock. His breath clips. He's holding back, being strong for me. I can still taste the salt off that shirt, feel the warmth of his lips through its gauze. Ya habibi, ya hayete, do you know it's the last time we're ever going to stand this close?

"I'll be right back," he whispers. "Be ready for me."

He steps out into the light and fades into the dust. It was as bright outside that morning as the sun is today over Mount Royal, with as much cement dust along the street as there is now snow on the dead leaves. I squint. And then the door closes behind him.

"Mama," Omar pulls at my jacket. "Let's go up. I want to see the city from the top, with all the snow covering it."

We continue along the gravel path to where the stairs begin their ascent to the lookout point. Those stairs are endless, and by the time we reach the top I'm panting like a dog. But the view is worth it. From up there, we can see all of Montreal. The office towers of downtown, the port district after the Bonaventure Expressway, and beyond that the St. Lawrence River.

"Look," I say, pointing, "there are three bridges."

"What's on the other side?"

"I don't know, habibi. More Montreal."

I love coming up here, even though I'm too tired to find the time most weeks. Up here, there's nothing to block the sky in all directions, and just looking at the city this way makes it a little easier to breathe. I too become un-obstructed without all the streets and buildings to make traffic, crowds and wind tunnels. We look through the big metal binoculars stationed around the lookout, and we can see what must be the United States on the horizon. At least that's what I hear another couple say as they stand next to us at the lookout.

It reminds me of Kfar Mechki in the mountains, where it never gets this cold. I wonder if I'll ever go back there again. It seems so far away. For four months I've had no news from home, nor have I written. The few times I've tried to call, all I ever get is a busy signal or a dead line. The war has taken down too many phone lines, and no one in my family has my number. I should send it in a letter, but I don't know anyone traveling there who can deliver it. I should probably write one anyway. I mean to, but what is there to say? Inshallah they're worried about me. But maybe they don't even care. I was always the afterthought when I was young. I showed up too late, and my parents took the attitude that it was fine if I just hung around the edges. Back home, there were always people around, and I could never get away from them. Now I can't help but miss them, even if they don't miss me. Here, no one even looks at me; they're all afraid to meet my eye. People are polite when they have to speak to me. Otherwise they act as if I'm not there.

But as I look out at this city on a clear, windless day, the sun brightening up all its sharp edges in its fresh white coat of snow, I can't help but think how beautiful it can all be too. It's going to be lunchtime soon. The day is warming up and more people are starting to arrive, pushing along the edges of the balcony to look out, look down, and take many photos, which they'll then walk down to the underground city to develop at Black's or the Japan Camera Centre. Next week, they will sort through what comes back and find a few to send off to family in the letters that they mail, or they will store them in an album or put one in a frame and hang it, set it by a bedside or down the hall. Yaneh I would love to do that, start taking photos. If only I could afford a little camera, a small roll of film, and the cheapest development package.

We leave the lookout and continue walking toward the mountain lake, and Omar plays with branches in the forest along the way. I've never thought that I would want to keep or remember any of this. Watching all those amateur photographers, I can't remember a time, in fact, in the three years since Halim disappeared, that I've been able to think of myself that way, as someone who wants to remember and keep mementos of the past. I only think of myself as someone pushing through, enduring. I haven't kept anything from what's happened to us. Except for the horse that Halim carved, which I keep on the kitchen table so that it's always with us, in the middle of the apartment.

Omar doesn't feel well. He barely touches the chicken, yogurt and rice I made for dinner. I feel his brow. He's hot to the touch. Even though it's still Saturday, I'm worried that I can't afford to keep him home from school on Monday and miss a day of work. I bring him a glass of water and a spoonful of Panadol.

"Want to eat something else, ya habibi?" I look through the cupboard and fridge to see what's left of the food boxes from work. "There's a spaghetti here." I pull it out and bring it over to the couch to show him, hoping the picture on the box might kickstart his appetite.

He shrugs and stares blankly at the television. He's too washed out to even complain about an investigative report on the Iran-Contra scandal that can't possibly interest him. I go ahead and change the channel until I find something a little more compelling than the nightly news. There's an episode of *Knight Rider* on. We sit on the sofa and I stroke his hair as we watch Michael tell KITT what to do and KITT reverses off the bed of the black truck and speeds off down the highway in the other direction, his custom panel full of blinking computer lights. Yaneh, for a boy it's a little more interesting than Reagan and Khomeini.

During the commercial break, Omar finally says, "I don't feel so good, Mama."

"I know, Mama. I'll take care of you. You have a fever, that's all. Inshallah, the Panadol should work soon."

I want nothing more than to calm him, but privately I'm second-guessing myself. I let him run off and play in the snow all day. His gloves and socks were soaked and freezing by the time we got back to the apartment. That's my fault. I kiss his brow. I bought him all the wrong clothes because I had no way of knowing how to dress for weather like this. I don't know what I'm doing. And now all I can do is offer Omar my affection while he pays the price for my mistakes.

I send him to bed early and leave a tall glass of water on his nightstand. As a baby, he used to get fevers all the time, and Halim and I would worry all through the night about where to find medicine. But the poor kid hasn't had a fever in years. I thought that kind of worry was all behind us now, as part of our old lives.

After Omar finally falls asleep, I quietly pull open the sofa bed and turn the TV on, to a station with a talk show. What a long day it's been. Ya rabi, I can't help but feel the weekends are harder. I'm sitting on the bed's edge, and I'm too tired to get up, wishing I still smoked, as my head drifts along to the images. It's difficult to understand the slangs and intonations of the French they speak here. I can follow the news or some of the English shows that have been dubbed in France, but when it comes to the talk shows, the dramas, and the comedies, the language relaxes and begins to sway and slur in expressions I can't follow. Smallah! Lise Carbonneau laughs and jokes this way when she speaks to the other pure laines. I am outside the intimacy that knowing those jokes creates. When I try to replicate it, I sound stiff and limited, like Khomeini talking down to Reagan.

When I'm not at work, I find myself thinking about Lise more than I should. She has such grace, poise, articulation, a theatrical flare that commands a room. Wherever Lise is, she's the center of that place.

Do I want to be Lise Carbonneau? I imagine myself walking from desk to desk in a smart pencil skirt, with important folders in my arms. I'll stop in at Marie-Hélène's cubicle, sit on the edge of her desk and share some anecdotes on last night's episode of that comedy *Manon*, a miniseries that follows the daily lives of the doctors, nurses, and administrators at a CLSC. All the women in the office love it. As Lise, I'll say something funny that Muna would never understand, and Marie-Hélène will laugh and lean forward as I set my warm hand on her shoulder. *See you at the four o'clock meeting, ma chérie.* Or *Have a good morning.* Then I'll move on to the next employee, working my way around the office with tact and class, amiably ensuring everything hums along to my exacting standards. It's impressive, the way she makes those rounds.

Sitting on the edge of the sofa bed, I drift off like this to the flickering images, thinking about nothing and everything, until I hear Omar stirring in the next room. Is he calling me or talking in his sleep? Quietly I get up and go stand outside the door to his room, listening. I peer in. It doesn't sound as if he's awake, just uncomfortable. I hear him tossing and turning in the dark. He's dreaming, I realize. *Aaaah*, he moans. *Waaa* ... What's he saying? *Naaaa* ... The poor thing. Should I wake him? Then I hear him call out, but I can only gasp when it's not to me. *Baaa ... Baaa. Baba. Weynak?*

He's calling for his father. Since we moved, Omar has never mentioned him once. I didn't think he thought much about Halim anymore. He cried a lot when it first happened, my mother told me, when I was so unsettled myself that I couldn't get out of bed for a month.

Yaneh, I always think of that whenever I catch our past problems percolating up through his innocence, that I've always failed him when he needed me. His baba is suddenly gone, to where no one can explain, and so his mama disappears into a bedroom. For a long time I couldn't fight my sadness. It was as though I were encased in it, like someone had placed me in a barrel and poured concrete and left me to dry. I could not see the point in getting out of bed or answering a simple question. I lay like that for six weeks at one point.

I look at Omar now, reaching out through his fever dream, his face hot, the heat connecting him to memories he doesn't even know he's kept, and I remember those days back in 1984 when he would come to lie beside me and kiss my wet face and beg me to get better. He thought it was his fault that I was sad. I kissed him when he begged me, as I cried harder, and I genuinely tried to smile through all those tears and lie to him, say things like "Don't worry, habibi. What's happening to me, it's not your fault. Mama's not sad, just tired. Mama needs her sleep."

I can't believe that was only two years ago. Ya Allah, I don't recognize that person or what she had to go through or the grief she suffered. I'm better now, more pragmatic about unfairness, more resigned to letting my ambitions go, kept afloat by an air bubble of numbness in the part of my chest where that love was torn out of me.

"Wake up, ya hayete." I say, gently shaking his arm. "Tell me, what are you feeling?"

He moans himself awake and realizes he's been trapped in a bad dream. Its spell finally broken, he cries in my arms. This time, I hold him close and rock him back and forth, reverting instinctively to the motion I used to lull him to sleep when he was a baby. "There there, my light, the love of my heart, sleep, nothing happened, it was all a bad dream, you're safe, I'm here." I plant my lips on his forehead, offer reassurance, affirmation, security. I take his temperature, which has gone down. His brow feels cooler. The Panadol is working. "Yallah, let's lie down and sleep."

Exhausted, Omar obeys.

After a few minutes, I get up, making sure he doesn't stir. From the doorway, I check on him one last time, and then I walk into the bathroom, where I undress, look at myself in the mirror with no special acknowledgement of the worn-down woman who looks back at me, and then climb into the shower, turn on the hot water, and once the temperature's set to exactly where I want it, when the water begins to feel like a womb, I cry into my palms. Under the shower's waterfall, I squint, sniffle, choke. I cough. I stutter my way through every defeated sound I know, and I hate myself for making them. I hope no one can hear me, and that the shower will keep my secret. I cry like that until I have nothing left in me, until I've been emptied, and then I stop and decide that it's over, that I should stop feeling sorry for myself. That I've already held myself together for this long. That I can't break apart again now.

Pruned, my olive skin pink and warm, I step out of the shower and wipe the steam from the mirror so I can see my eyes. I want to see them laid bare and bloodshot, beaten, surrendered. I stare at them, staring back at me. As the mirror begins to steam over again, I see Halim transpire behind my shoulder. I can feel his breathing along the nape of my neck, the almost feeling of having a body I know so close to my touch. I feel a soft electricity where his hands hover just above my shoulders.

"Weynak?" I ask him. "Where are you, my heart? He needs you. I need you."

In the white steam of the tiny bathroom, Halim says nothing. I close my eyes and focus on his proximity. His presence feels stronger if I hold my breath. I want so badly to feel the imprint of hands, their tentativeness, their confidence, their embrace around my waist as I turn and fall in. And then, for a moment, I do. I turn around with my eyes closed and am met only by the towel hanging on the wall behind me. I let my breath go, open my eyes, and Halim is gone.

"I wanted to tell you that this isn't the right place for me," I say, still feeling the residue of his company. "I made a mistake coming here without you."

I feel better for saying it, and for not feeling so alone in that moment. Who in this city cares about me bending the truth just a little?

To the light of the TV, I put on my pajamas and brush my hair and teeth before climbing into bed. The news anchor is calling the night's lottery numbers. The prize tonight is 1.3 million dollars. Who would be the lucky person to win that? I imagine myself in the sofa bed piled high with twenty-dollar bills, the winner. Smallah, I smile.

It's now the middle of December, and that snow that comes down lightly, like in a storybook? Yaneh, it only showed up two more times before transforming into something else entirely. For the past night and day, an icier, more abusive sleet has been raining down and hardening into glass along the sidewalks.

I've never seen so much of it, never felt so much of it attacking my face, like little stings. I raise my meager scarf to cover my eyes. It's a quarter to eight in the morning, and I'm walking Omar to school. We lean in for balance and to protect our exposed skin. Even though I can hardly afford it, after his fever broke, I bought Omar new mitts and a neck warmer to better fill the gaps in his snowsuit. And good that I did, because he would have frozen during this storm. On TV they're calling it the first storm of the season. We've learned our lesson, my little apricot, I think as I kiss him goodbye. From now on, I'll dress you as if we're heading out onto the surface of the moon.

By the time I make it to the office, I find a new notice on the announcement board. Lise Carbonneau has called a morning meeting. I join the dozen other saleswomen in the conference room, where a few chat but most sit quietly. Now that I've been here a month, I see how quickly people turn over. The Monday after I collected my first paycheck, almost half the sales team disappeared. A few got fired for not selling enough, one person got a better job and moved on, and the rest just stopped showing up without giving a reason. A new batch of phone people has come in to replace them. Of the people who were on the floor when I first began, now only six remain. It's better if I don't get invested in any of these people. I'll move on too, the second a teaching position comes my way. I nod silent approval to that thought, even if I find it harder and harder to believe in.

Lise walks in, dressed once again in Christmas colors: a red angora-wool sweater with poofy shoulders, a green pleated skirt, and white tights. I like the sweater a lot, and as she sets up her slides at the front, I wonder if I might find something like it on the discount floor at The Bay after the holidays, when prices go down. It looks like a Christmas sweater in December, but come January it will look just like any other red sweater.

At the beginning of the month, Lise announced that Christmas was her favorite holiday. "You can expect me to celebrate it all month long, and bien sûr I encourage you to do so as well!" She had been true to her word; she had not missed a day. I've come to look forward to seeing the new outfit each morning. It's like she has a *Vogue* magazine for a closet. There's something a little ostentatious about Lise Carbonneau. I admire this about her. She's not afraid to act like a movie star, even though she works here.

Lise begins by announcing that she has good news. "Everyone on the sales team is getting two weeks off for the holidays, mes chéries! Go spend time with your families, rest, recharge, and we'll come back strong in January." Of course, she adds matter-of-factly, it will be unpaid. "But all your jobs are guaranteed to be here when you return."

With a clicker in hand, she dims the lights and guides us through her slideshow of statistics from past years that basically show no one wants to hear from a weight-loss consultant during the Christmas holidays, when families are gathered and wine flows and plates of food roll out from kitchens to feed aunts and uncles, grandparents and in-laws, cousins and kids. But starting in that first week of January, she stresses, we can expect to be busier than ever before. "Over the next few weeks, your regular clients will slide backward by an average five to ten pounds in their attempts to lose weight. The coldest months of the year are also the most desperate ones for weight management, when our clients feel most hopeless," Lise explains, pointing to the lowest ebb of a wave on a projected graph of hope's annual arc.

But two weeks without pay … I worry about that as I walk back to my desk. If I don't spend anything extra, then there's a chance I'll have enough left by month's end for the weekly rent. There you have it, Muna, all these holidays are going to do is to eat away at what little savings you have left. I'm looking at the boxes on my desk, always there, always egging me to make the next sale, and in my head I'm calculating how many I can take home between now and the break. A lot of phone consultants here never touch them. I'd be helping them look more engaged by taking their boxes too. Just to save a little extra until January.

It's time to get on the phone and start making my calls. This morning, I'm checking in with clients I've spoken to before. I'm scheduled to call Sylvie Leduc, forty-six, from Brossard on the South Shore. Sylvie was passed down to me from the previous phone consultant. Her name was in the blue binder when I was first assigned this desk. We've spoken twice so far. She's a full-time mother, and I have it marked down that this is a good time to call: her two boys are at school, her husband at the office.

The phone rings twice before she picks up.

"Oui, allô?"

"Sylvie, bonjour, it's Mona from Nutri-Fort. How are you?"

I hear hesitation in her silence. Then she says, "I'm okay, Mona. And you?"

"Not bad," I say, sensing I may have caught her at a bad time. "Looking forward to the holidays?"

"Sure, pourqoui pas." Sylvie chuckles to what may be a TV show in the background. "Do you like the holidays? I look around at all the shop windows and watch all the Christmas specials on the TV, and I love the feeling they create. But in my own life, the holidays feel more like pressure than joy."

I can hear frustration building in her voice. "We have a lot of expectations placed on us, it's true," I say.

"The list is endless: call people, extend invitations, write cards, talk on the phone, make plans, cancel plans.

Between you and me, crisse, I'll breathe a sigh of relief when it all ends. I don't even like these people. It's all Jean-Marc's family, Jean-Marc's friends, Jean-Marc's coworkers. "

"It really is the busiest season of all, isn't it?" I say, thinking back to one of Lise's slides about staying on subject. "So many things to do. Did you get my last package, Sylvie?"

"I sure did. I've dedicated one cupboard and half a shelf in the fridge just for my boxes. Tes boîtes digestives, my sons tease me. They think I'm doing this all to go to the bathroom. This is what it's like in a house with three boys."

"I thought you said you had two."

"Well, Jean-Marc's not much better. Can I ask you something, Mona? Just between us girls? Do you know what it means when a man is there but he isn't there?"

I hold my breath, unsure whether to follow her into this more personal territory. "Yes, I think I do."

"Like his body is physically there, at the dinner table chewing loudly, snoring next to me in bed, walking ahead of me at the mall. But somewhere along the way, I can sense that *he* is not there, even though I still get the part of him that burps and farts."

"You mean emotionally."

"C'est ça, Mona. I mean engaged. There."

I want to ask, *Well where do you think he is?* but it strikes me as too personal a question, so instead I say, "What does Jean-Marc think of your weight-loss plan?"

Sylvie snorts. "He doesn't care. He says, 'Even if you lose the weight, you'll still be old.' As if I promised him I'd stay nineteen forever the moment he got me pregnant.

Like it's my fault that we got older or that he became responsible for something more than a bowl of chips to go with his Labatt's."

"I hope you don't let that discourage you, Sylvie. You know, we take care of our bodies for ourselves, not for others."

"I know, Mona. But it's more than not caring. Before I began the program, he couldn't care less about anything I did. But now, I think he's threatened that I have a project for myself. When I serve him and the boys their dinner and then prepare my own meal separately, he says things like, *Playing with your boxes again?* Or, *Our food's not good enough for you?* Our food! As if he would know how to make any of the dishes he insists we eat. They're the reason I gained the weight in the first place. *Make more meat, make more sauce, you call this a portion!* He wants me to fail."

"What is your weight this week?"

"Two hundred twenty. But before you say anything, I know it's up. It's just, right now with everything I have to do to get ready for the holidays, I can't deal with him making fun of me for eating the boxes at dinner. The boys are starting to get in the habit of doing it too. It's too much. I'm just eating a smaller portion of what I make them, to keep the peace. I don't pay him any attention when he badgers me to have seconds."

"Sylvie, I'm so sorry to hear it's like this in your home right now. Our homes are like extensions of our bodies. In fact, wouldn't you agree we spend more time looking after our homes than we do ourselves?"

"Mais oui, but it's easy to buy a new carpet or put up

new curtains. We share the home. It's not just mine. It's not like buying myself new shoes."

"But your family all agrees it must be cared for. You choose new silverware just as you fix the toilet. Your love for the home is both a beautifying and a maintenance. Love for your home only works if it includes love for everyone in it. Sylvie, can I be open with you, can I speak with you woman to woman?"

"Please, Mona," I hear her say. "I have no one else."

"Would it be wrong for me to say that if your husband's behavior toward you improved . . ."

"Everything would be so much easier." She sighs.

"So we agree. The problem is not you. Don't see yourself as the problem. Even if Jean-Marc doesn't love you like he once did, he still needs to treat you like he would treat any friend or colleague on the street. Sylvie, the boxes of food, they're just a Band-Aid, ma chérie. Talk to your husband, calmly. It's important he knows you want to be treated with respect. You cannot carry the blame for feeling the way you do and wanting to fix it."

"You're right, Mona," she says. I can hear her weeping on the other end of the line. I stay quiet, letting her have the moment to shed some tears while someone else listens. Even if I can't be there for her, in the room, my hand on her shoulder, I can still be there as a voice that agrees, that lets her know she's not all alone. It's the first time I've ever had a caller go this far. I'm not sure I'm supposed be so open with a client, but I can't sit here all day, every day, listening to these stories and not raise a hand or say something in return.

"Sylvie, it's important to stand up for yourself," I say to her, "even if it can feel sometimes like no one else cares."

"Does anyone ever care about the mother?" she says, tearing up.

"Motherhood is not your sacrifice to the family but your gift. Without you there is no center to the home, no one to cook *or* to care."

"Without me, this whole place would fall apart. They'd be three pigs living in their own filth."

"You must take care of yourself, if only to continue to care for them. Tell Jean-Marc that it's important for you to do this. The boxes are not for him or anyone else to worry about. Tell him not to get in your way. It doesn't involve him doing a thing. It's about respecting you. Tell him you don't want your sons getting the example that they can talk to a woman the way he talks to you."

"You're right, Mona. You're so right. I'll try that."

"You can do it, when you're ready. Tu es capable."

Before Sylvie wonders if she should have an answer for that, I pivot back to the holidays, and we finish up by preparing a meal plan for the next three weeks. After exchanging a few more pleasantries about the holidays, we schedule our next call for January. I hang up.

With my elbows on my desk, I hold my head in my hands and take a deep breath. I exhale. I count to ten and I sit back up. I'm afraid I've been too forward. What if, after she calms down and thinks about it, Sylvie Leduc comes to her senses and decides I tricked her into revealing too much about herself on a call with a stranger? I spoke to her as I would a sister. She spoke to Mona. I wonder if Sylvie

Leduc would talk to me about these things if she knew who I really am. Muna Heddad, the foreigner who can't even ask people for directions on Sherbrooke without them quickening their pace to outrun her. The one nobody will put in front of a classroom. The one who can barely hold on to an apartment for her own son to sleep in this holiday.

I get up from my desk to stretch my legs. In the office kitchen, I make myself a tea in the microwave. It's gray outside today, frozen. I look south, to the river and the bridges. The traffic below, along rue de la Gauchetière, honks and breaks as the lunch hour approaches. I sit down at the table by the window and leaf through the September issue of *Vogue*, numbly coasting through photo shoots in the French Alps and ads for lipstick. This is Lise's old copy. She has a subscription, I've learned, and whenever a new issue shows up in the mail, she's kind enough to let us read the old ones before they end up in the trash.

I wipe away the steam from the bathroom mirror. I see that my lids are perpetually dark, always heavy, bloodshot from the air indoors now that no one opens the windows. Apart from my twice-daily walk to and from the Nutri-Fort office, I'm hardly ever outdoors anymore. All I breathe is whatever's left over from other people breathing in the buildings, metro, and underground city. I can taste its staleness on my tongue, the ghosts of all those abu reihas down my throat. I can see it in these crow's feet, faint but now permanent, etching arcs around each eye. My skin is no longer that of the girl who went to teachers college.

"Do you remember those days?" I say, closing my eyes and allowing the bathroom's steam to open my pores and comb out the grime of a day's movements. These stolen moments have become something I look forward to, a secret back door into being able to share an intimate moment, a cheat when no one's paying attention.

"I do," I hear Halim whisper behind me, his warm breath blowing ever so gently against the back of my neck. "You would drop Omar off at your sister's, go to class, study in the library before you came back home. You were always moving, a million things to do."

"Some things don't change," I say. "I've been ignoring him for his whole life. I'm a bad mother." I let myself rest back against his chest, as his fingers massage my shoulders. "I'm so tired all the time. You're lucky to be gone."

"I would do anything to be here with you. I would do anything to help."

"What if that's not true?" I whisper. "What if you became more like Jean-Marc? What if, over the years, you grew stifled by our marriage and its responsibilities? What if you began to hate me for it?"

"Jean-Marc is fooling himself by blaming Sylvie for his unhappiness. Some blame others and never look at themselves."

"I don't want you to blame me. I'm doing the best I can. This was your idea."

"Without you, I'm nothing. You are my thoughts, just as I am yours. We are two vines, entwined."

"Only one of us has wilted dry and the other is still caught twisted in …"

"My stranglehold?"

"Your embrace."

In the steam of the tiny bathroom, before the door re-opens and the cold rushes back in and melts the heat away, Halim wraps his arms around my waist and presses me toward him.

Am I not allowed warmth, a direct connection to a comforting hand? I know, from the phone calls at work, that some married women talk to the men in their lives this way even when their husbands are ignoring them from the next room over. Would I feel this way if you were not gone but parked in front of the television, the dishes from an unappreciated supper still waiting at the table for a more feminine hand than yours to come along and wash them? Would you still be grateful if I did this for you every night?

"Good night," I say, kissing his hand. "I'm tired and tomorrow's a long day."

Halim kisses my shoulder and fades away as I push open the bathroom door and the hot air siphons out. Wrapped in a towel, I step out into the living room and let the winter dampness that's trapped in our apartment cool me down as I comb out my hair and then slip on my nightgown. I walk over to the kitchen and pour myself a glass of milk to wash down all the film of office air still caught in my chest.

The pullout bed is already open and made. I lie down for the first time that day and lose myself to the beginnings of a black-and-white movie on Radio-Canada. Ya-neh, I'm not blind. I know there's a Jean-Marc hiding inside every Halim. I know we had our blissful summer in Kfar Mechki, lost in the mountains before everyone knew about us. But after that we were never warm like this, romantic. After that, it was one pressure after another: his arranged marriage, the war, my father's negotiations, his mother's suspicions, the cellars, the kidnapping. I know that I'm bending a person's memory to keep myself together, because no one else here will. But I haven't forgotten how he would become preoccupied with his older brothers. He could bristle over a veiled insult for days. Every once in a while, he was capable of sitting at our kitchen table for an entire afternoon, as I fed Omar, complaining about something a neighbor had said in the storage rooms the night before. Politicians and their promises fed his diatribes whenever a glass of arak was on the table. He could get so upset sometimes. I wonder if, over the years and with nothing extraordinary to stop him, every Halim turns into a Jean-Marc.

The movie is silly, some more men acting like clowns for easy laughs. On the screen, a man tries to jump over an elephant using a long pole and falls flat on his face in the process. A lot of the time, men are just donkeys who imagine themselves as horses. Everyone laughs. I turn off the TV.

The holiday season. Back home we never make a big show of it like they do here. Here, from the first of December the entire downtown is decorated in Christmas's honor, the stores and the streets alike, and even our office has a little silver-needled tree in the reception area. In two weeks, it has already collected some presents under it. Every morning and every evening as I pass by, I wonder if those presents are real. I never stoop down to pick one up to find out. It's better to pretend that someone in the office is getting a gift than to know the boxes are just empty decorations.

In Beirut, December is a gray, uneventful month. Maybe it rains. The fighting in the streets usually settles down as the lazy soldiers start shivering in their hideouts inside other people's abandoned apartments and return to their mothers' tables for something warm to eat. Christmas Eve is a somber occasion, a night to have a meal with family and then go to church and light candles. During the war, Christmas Eve was one of the few times in the year when all the militias would take a break because snipers and checkpoint guards have families too. They would trade holidays so everyone could celebrate their religion's special days. The fighting had gone on for so long that a ritual of respect and hospitality began to infiltrate their hatred for one another.

No one even thinks of giving gifts. The pause in fighting is just long enough to go to the church with flashlights and candles in hand. We pass other families along the way, exchange pleasantries. Halim, Omar, and I would arrive at the church's square, which would be strung up with lights connected to a generator for the evening. Christmas mass was just another sign of another year ending. We had no inclination to look back fondly. Inshallah next year would be better. I used to think it couldn't possibly get any worse, and then Halim was kidnapped. I haven't celebrated the last two Christmases at all.

And now I'm here, wondering if there's anything in those boxes under the silver tree at work. Of all the changes that have happened this year, this is the one I least expected: the decorated tall evergreens on McGill's campus, the carols spilling out from all the speakers in the underground city, the costumed Santas entertaining lineups of children in the department stores. They all remind me that I'm in a new world, that my past is gone and I have permission to move on. It's bittersweet to know that moment has come.

Our first Christmas on our own. No family to call on, no neighbors to randomly drop in. What will we do? I should get Omar a present.

It's mild out this evening, and I'm walking home along Sainte-Catherine Street, where the sidewalks are crowded with shoppers pushing past and bright lights blinking. At the street corner, there's a lot of construction happening and a giant sign says there'll be a new underground shopping center opening soon, Promenades Cathédrale. The plows have dug a large hole into the lawn of the Christ Church Cathedral behind it, which I only now see is giving its name to the shopping center that will live underneath. On what's left of the church's lawn, there's a sign advertising a Christmas Eve mass. ALL ARE WELCOME, it reads in big black letters. Ya rabi, everything here is a commercial. Still, it's not that far from the apartment, and if the weather isn't too cold that night ... It all depends on how we feel that day.

Back at the apartment building, there's even a tree in the lobby now.

"Where do people get those?" I ask Mr. Saltzman. He's placing notices in mailboxes.

"What, the trees? They're everywhere."

"Are they expensive?"

He looks at me like I'm joking, and then he says, "Right, you're new here. You know what, people leave them behind all the time. I've got a few down in the storage. If you want, I'll lend you one."

"Really? That would be great. Let me just go upstairs, put my things down and check on my son. I'll be back down in a minute."

He turns his back to me and continues pushing notices into the mailboxes. Over the past few months I've learned this is his way of saying okay.

I take the elevator upstairs and find Omar parked on the sofa, watching TV. There's a channel, MusiquePlus, that plays only music videos all day, and he's been watching that a lot lately. The videos are flashy and quick, the hosts are young and cool, and I don't mind because to me it's just like having a radio on in the apartment. Plus, I've walked past their headquarters on Sainte-Catherine before, and I always get tingles whenever I peer through their blackened windows to see what's going on inside. Every once in a while on TV, you can see someone doing just that.

"How was school today?" I kiss the top of his head as I take off my heavy coat.

He shrugs, not taking his eyes off the screen, where a sweaty man sits in a small apartment like this one, with sunglasses twisting in his fingers as he sings about wearing sunglasses at night.

"Okay, good," I say, rolling my eyes at how the music videos captivate him. "Yallah, I have to go downstairs to talk to Mr. Saltzman. I'll be back soon and we'll have dinner."

Instead of acknowledging me, he laughs at how determined the singer looks, walking around the streets at night with sunglasses on, and I take that to mean he's not that hungry. This boy really needs his few hours to deflate after coming home from school, I've noticed. I hope it's not a sign of a bad habit forming. Ya rabi, one problem at a time.

I take the elevator downstairs, thinking a Christmas tree will be the thing to capture Omar's attention and pull him away from the TV that's always on now that he spends so much time home alone. Mr. Saltzman is back in his office watching the six o'clock news on the little black-and-white TV on his desk. They're everywhere, these TVs, wherever I go. He sees me coming and reaches into his drawer to pull out a heavy key chain.

"Come on," he waves as he passes me. "It's this way."

I follow Mr. Saltzman down the corridor behind his glass-walled office. At the end of the hall, he opens the door labeled LAUNDRY and leads me down the stairwell I already know too well. The laundry room is the first door to the left. Two machines are spinning, and along the table in the back a tenant is folding a pile of clothes.

"You have a lot of foreign students in this building," I say, just to say something at all.

"Nature of the location," he says as we continue down the hall. "We're right next to the university gates, and the foreigners are more interested in living high up in apartments. Unlike the Canadian kids, who prefer the older duplexes and triplexes with roommates and yards. Plus, these foreign kids are quiet. They pay their rent and the rest of the time, they study."

We stop at a door at the end of the hall, and Mr. Saltzman pulls out his large ring of keys, which he has attached to an extendable chain on his belt. He files through the many keys like a Rolodex, and I stare off at the corner, because I know from past experience there's no use trying to rush an old man already set in his habits. When he finds the one he's looking for, he unlocks the door, gives it a gentle push, and we enter. He turns on the lights. There are boxes everywhere, on the floor, on the numerous tables, on the shelves, on the chairs and sofas and beds that fill the large, low-ceilinged room. Between them, wherever a free surface lies available, there are lamps, vases, and countertop appliances, old TVs, radios, abandoned books. I can almost see myself hiding behind these bookshelves or stowed between the stacks of boxes, as I used to do in the cellar of our building in Ashrafieh whenever the bombing came too close.

"There's so much of everything," I say, looking around as I follow Mr. Saltzman down a jagged, narrow aisle between furniture pieces. "Where do you get all this from? It's like a store down here."

"It's the kids. They rent here for a few years while they study, their parents send them with old furniture, or they buy stuff and have no one to give it to when they move back home, or they find an armchair on the street and bring it up, and when they leave, they can't be bothered. Sometimes I'll even find a nice piece out on the curb and I'll bring it down here."

"I can't believe they leave this all behind." I'm marveling at the quality of a vase to my right. It practically looks like crystal. "Some of these things are so expensive."

"They're kids," he shrugs. "What do you want, for them to be responsible? Most of them are happy to leave. They get jobs or get married, move back home or travel."

"Lucky them," I say absently, as I peruse the spines of some books and then feel the weight of a skillet right next to them.

"If you ever need anything, just ask me, Ms. Heddad. I have this key." He holds it up and smiles. "It's not easy where you are, I know. Feel free to take what you want. It's all collecting dust anyway. Whether here or upstairs, it doesn't matter."

"Oh that's very generous of you, Mr. Saltzman. Thank you."

"My parents did what you're doing now. I was little, like your son, when I first got here. It was a different city then."

"When was that?"

"After the war, the Second World War. For the first five years we were here, we lived in an apartment with two other families, me, my parents, my two brothers, my sister, and my aunt all living in bunks in one room that had this little sink and stove. Back then you had to go to the bathroom in the hall. You have it easy, Ms. Heddad."

"I suppose it looks that way, yes," I say. "I'll have to keep that in mind."

"My father went on to do very well for himself. He made connections, bought this building. I'm not saying this to brag or anything. I'm just telling you the story. Mostly I get kids here. I have to call their parents for the rent. But you, I could see you really needed it, and so I took a chance. I know the other landlords won't rent to you. They see an immigrant and throw up application forms to say someone else got the place. They see your skin and worry you'll make the place stink. They see a single mom and fear there'll be strange men coming and going. They see a kid and they say there'll be too much noise. It sounds like I'm being rude, sorry, but I see all kinds in this business, let me tell you. You get a knack for people. You looked decent enough and at the end of your rope, so I took a chance."

"You're very kind to not assume the worst." Yaneh, I'm not really sure what else to say to a man who has never spoken to me this long before. Everyone wants to talk now.

I think he means well. In my experience, old men will say whatever they're thinking, regardless of who's listening.

"Here are the trees," Mr. Saltzman says.

We're at the very back of the storage room. There's a cage along the back wall that resembles the one Halim, Omar, and I used to sleep in back in Beirut. Using another of his keys, he unlocks it and we enter the dusty concrete-floored space where dozens of plastic Christmas trees rest in a pile against the wall. I stand back as Mr. Saltzman digs into the pile, pulling out trees and setting them aside as he looks for one to lend me.

"Here, try this one. It should be a good size. You have to do a little assembly."

"Is it hard to do?"

"Nah, it's just a few pieces. You'll figure it out. Wish I could give you some decorations too, but those tend to break so they just end up in the garbage. Still, it's enough to get you started for your first Christmas here. Enjoy it, Ms. Heddad, it'll only go downhill from there."

"What do you mean, Mr. Saltzman?"

"This is an easy city to love leading up to the holidays, but after that, it's dark and cold like the Arctic until April. Be ready, is all I'm telling you. I remember from when I was a boy. It hurts those first few years. But then you get used to it, you'll see."

"Well, thank you for this."

"Ms. Heddad, may I ask you a personal question?"

"Okay ..."

"Where's the boy's father?"

Gazing down at the place in the cage where we once

slept, now crowded with artificial trees, I pause for a moment and think of how to best explain where Halim could be at this moment. "He's dead, Mr. Saltzman. We lost him to the war in Lebanon two years ago. Almost three now, come to think of it."

"Of course. I'm so sorry for your loss." The color falls out of his face, and now he's embarrassed that he's ventured too far. He sighs. "Unfortunately," he adds, "my family knows a few things about living with those ghosts. Listen, do you need anything else? Anything that's down here, it's just taking up space. Look around. Or down the road, if you need something for the apartment, come ask me for the key. Anyway, take your time. I'll come back and lock up a little later."

Mr. Saltzman leaves me alone in the storage room with the old furnishings of so many other strangers who've moved on with their lives. I walk slowly through the aisles, looking at a set of dishes here, a vacuum there. Will I move on too, or am I different? Will I get stuck because of all those excuses Mr. Saltzman recited to me? He thought he was offending me, but he's right. I see it everywhere around me, when we were first looking for a place to live, while I was looking for work, when I shop at stores in the underground mall, when I'm walking home from the office in the evening, if I'm on the metro. Maybe it means that this is the best I can expect. Poor Halim, he would have been so disappointed by all these invisible obstacles. I look back to the cage half-expecting him to be there, nodding in agreement, but there's no one there.

"I'm sorry, ya habibi," I say. "I didn't mean to tell him

you're dead. It just would have been too hard to explain anything else."

I remember that I'm leaving Omar alone for too long, again, and so I begin to move toward the door, carrying the small Christmas tree under my arm. I spot a game of Monopoly that appears to be in good shape. Is he too young for the game? I don't even know how to play, but he'll like that he's seen the commercials on TV. I take the Monopoly for now, and maybe I can come back later for a more thorough search.

Unlocking our apartment door, I see Omar still parked on the couch, lost to the TV. I quietly set the board game in the hall closet before I say anything. Once it's stowed away, I make an exaggerated straining sound as I heave the tree into the living room and block his view of the screen.

"Look what I found."

He perks up. "What is it?"

"A Christmas tree."

"Yay!" He leaps off the couch, runs around the coffee table, and falls down on his knees to inspect the tree. "Can we put it together now?"

"Of course, ya mama," I say, rubbing the top of his head for good luck. "Then I'll make us some dinner."

We begin folding out the branches to see what the bundle of wire looks like. Set up, it stands as tall as my waist.

"Does it have decorations?" he asks.

"Yaneh, that's where I need your help. Your job is to make some."

"How?"

How, I wonder, fearing I've backed myself into a false promise. "With the food boxes from work. We won't throw them in the garbage. We'll cut them up and color them and hang them from the tree."

"And does that mean I'll get a present too? The other kids at school won't stop talking about getting presents for their trees, and I've never had a tree or a present, so now that I have a tree ..."

"You can have a present," I finish his sentence.

He runs at me and wraps his arms around my waist and hugs me tighter than he's hugged me in a long time. Ya rabi, it's because he's hugging me out of happiness for the first time. I let him hold me as he imagines out loud what kind of present he wants. I'll stand here and stroke his hair and let the moment last as long as possible.

My last day before the two-week holiday break, it's half past eleven in the morning and I'm at my desk, and outside it's snowing, real snow, the kind that makes me realize what I saw before was just a beginning. The snow coming down today doesn't look like it will melt away for a long time. When I passed her office door earlier, I heard Lise Carbonneau joking on a call – "Nous rentrons dans la congélateur, asti!" I thought it was so clever how she was talking about "entering the freezer," but she said it in such a way that you understood she was also talking about our unpaid leave – *congé*lateur. Smallah, I thought to myself as I walked past, that's exactly the kind of gymnastics I'll never master with the French they speak here.

I stare at the sales report in front of me, but I don't know if I'm even reading it. I just have my head down for a few minutes to sip this bland coffee in peace before my next call. This congé has me concerned about money, but in another sense I'm also relieved. Omar is going to be out of school for that time, and I won't have to leave him at home alone. Also, I'm tired. This endless year, I've realized, is finally coming to an end! If we don't leave the apartment for the entire two weeks, it will be the first rest I've gotten since our flight touched down at Mirabel airport in August. We can just sit in our congélateur and watch cable TV. I've bought a bag of rice and a bag of chickpeas and a bag of potatoes and bag of onions. I even found a tub of tahini in a small store in the underground city during my lunch break one day. It was expensive, but I can make it last for a month. Yaneh, sesame paste is the only flavor I've found here that tastes like home.

Finishing my coffee, I return to my list to see who to call next. It's Louis Laflamme. I like Louis. I can already see that he's on the program more for the phone calls than the diet. *Il répond bien à la touche humaine*, as Lise would say. I have to be his friend, while paying attention to the ratio that measures the number of calls and the length of each call. "There is an optimal balance," Lise always says. "Use the clock on your desk and start winding it down after ten minutes. You never want to end abruptly. It should be a staged comedown: looking forward, orders for more boxes, a manageable to-do list, remind them to call if anything comes up."

Despite his bureaucratic job somewhere deep in the offices of the provincial electricity provider, Louis always has time to talk.

The phone rings twice before he picks up.

"Hydro Québec, department des comptes. Monsieur Laflamme à l'appareil."

"Bonjour, Louis. It's Mona, your nutritionist. How are you this morning?"

"Oh, Mona, I'm so happy to hear from you."

Ya albeh this makes me feel good even though it

shouldn't. He's single and his eating disorder stems from being much too isolated. I am a woman with a soft voice. "It's okay to play with that," Lise always says. "You'll only ever be a voice on the telephone."

"Christmas is coming!" I beam as I say this. For the month of December, this is the best segue into any number of issues the customer wants to raise. "Do you have plans for the holidays?"

"Oh, I don't take much time off." I hear him chuckling on the other end as he speaks in a low voice, the tone people use at work when they're on personal calls. "Just the statutory days. I don't really have anyone to see, so I might as well keep busy."

"Good for you. The world needs more people like you to make sure the lights stay on. Did you get the package I sent you?"

"Mais oui. I had the chicken pot pie one for supper last night. It was delicious."

"Isn't it? I like to combine it with the chocolate pudding cup for a nice little dessert."

"I'll do that," he agrees. I make a note to send along a few extra chocolate puddings.

"Did you weigh yourself this week?"

"Mm-hmm."

"And?"

"Two forty-three. Down two pounds."

"That's fantastic, Louis. Oh, I'm so proud of you. How do you feel?"

"I feel good," he says. "Like you said, if I stick to the boxes, it's easier."

"That's right, it's one less thing to worry about."

"To be honest, one less thing makes all the difference."

"It's a hard time of year," I pivot. "Isn't it, Louis?"

"Oh, it's never easy. But yeah, now is tough."

"Do you have a few minutes? Tell me, what's on your mind?"

"Oh, you know, it doesn't really change. I'm just in my own head too much. Ever since my mother passed away, the house is empty. I wake up, I drive to the train station, I take the train, I sit at my desk all day doing the bookkeeping, and then I go home."

"No plans to take a vacation during the holidays, go somewhere warm?"

"I'd love it, don't get me wrong. But people my size don't sit well on planes or on beaches. Besides, I don't like the heat."

"Of course. And with this being the first Christmas without your mother …"

"It hurts, yeah. I miss her being there, even though I didn't like her much when she was there. Is that bad to say?"

"No, Louis, of course not. Nothing's bad to say," I reply, even as I wonder if that's true. "It's all very complicated how we feel about people, especially parents. Saying it out loud can help us make sense of it, don't you think? Put the thought in its rightful place."

"It's just now that she's gone, all I hear is her nagging in my head all the time. At least when she was alive I could shut her out."

We talk for a while about the kind of things his mother used to hassle him for.

"It's so hard to figure out what to do with these feelings when someone dies. You have to stay strong, Louis."

"I suppose you're right. But you know what? There are times when I look in the mirror and I hate what I see so much that it's all I can do to not cut myself," he says.

Ya rabi, I can't tell if M. Laflamme is trying to provoke me, or if he's crying out for help. For a moment, the line sits quiet as his words settle. If I let the pause continue too long, he'll feel even worse and then who knows where we'll end up.

"Of course you're not going to do that, Louis," I say with a little laugh. "Who else would I talk to?"

I'm relieved when he laughs. "You're right, Mona. I like these calls too."

"I want you to think of the diet as cutting yourself in a way that doesn't hurt," I say. "Take that bad thought and make it good."

"I'll do that, Mona. Thanks for sticking with me."

"So what's on the menu for this week?"

"Well, I'm going to have the pasta primavera tonight, and then I figured it's the weekend tomorrow, so I'm taking the chicken wings out of the freezer."

"Aren't those so good? Everyone deserves a treat, Louis. And as long as the calories on the boxes add up to twenty-one hundred by day's end, you'll lose weight. You'll see. One day you'll look in that mirror and a different man will be standing there, and he'll be the new you."

"I'm really looking forward to that day."

"I'm away for the next two weeks, but you can expect that I'll call you in January."

"Big holiday plans?"

"Not really. But I'm going to send along all your packages today to your pick-up location, to make sure you're set."

"No one takes better care of me," he jokes.

"Except you," I offer back. On the order form, I see that under dessert there's a special holiday cheesecake. "And I'm sending you a present this time too. It's tiny, but don't eat it all at once."

"Oh you're so nice, Mona. I wish I could send you a present too."

"We'll talk after the holidays. Joyeux noël, Louis."

I hang up, let out a sigh, and look at the clock. Fourteen minutes. Not bad. It felt longer than that, but I followed the script and it kept the conversation from going places it shouldn't. It's noon now, time for lunch. In the kitchen, I open one of the salad samples on the counter that needs to be eaten before it expires. I drizzle on the dressing pouch and then try to eat the hard croutons and limp greens without paying them much attention. I'm eating only to put something in my stomach so I won't be hungry. I wonder if Louis feels this way when he eats the food I sell him. Is it helping? Two pounds isn't much for a man his size. I worry his problem runs deeper than the solution I have to offer.

After I finish, I collect my purse and take the elevator down to the metro level, where I walk absently through the underground city's corridors as people push past and crowds swell whenever a train arrives. I'm not going to buy anything, but it's just distracting to get lost among

others at this time of year, when everyone is buying presents for the people in their lives. I look at the toy store
windows and hope Omar won't be too old for toys by
next Christmas, inshallah, when I can afford to buy him a
proper gift. For this year, the board game from the storage
room will have to do.

Playing Mona is harder with some clients than it is
with others. People pull me into their lives and beg me
to tell them what to do, and what can I say? What does
anyone say to a stranger who tells them he wants to cut
himself? Who reaches out to me for answers I don't have?
Whose world I don't even understand? Yaneh, I can't tell
him, *Listen, Louis, if you cut yourself no one will find you
and you'll die. But like your mother, you won't go away.
You'll live on in someone's thoughts, somewhere, maybe even
mine, just like your mother lives on in yours. And I can't
have your ghost in my head because I'm already carrying
around others, so many that I can barely keep up with them.
Eat all you want if it makes you happy. Your mother's not going away, but you can make peace with her rather than just
have her torment you. You can think of her as a companion
and not a haunting. Death is but one end. We have other
lives to live, but they look nothing like what we understand
of this one.*

I enter the clothing section of the Eaton's, and under
the bright lights I file through the racks of clothes, not
because I can afford any of these sweaters but because
it calms me, and if I'm honest with myself I would say
that the call with Louis has left me a little rattled, tense.
Sometimes I feel like I'm lonelier than all the the people

on the phones combined. Sometimes I think I'm absorbing them all, and they're turning me into someone I don't want to be.

After walking between the racks at the Eaton's for half an hour, I go back to my desk, dial the next call, and say, "Bonjour, Mona de Nutri-Fort à l'appareil. Comment vas-tu?"

Christmas Eve. Ya Allah, finally. The beginning of the end; seven more days for a year that's overstayed its welcome. I find it hard to imagine who I was even twelve months ago. While seated in the pew of the cathedral with the mall being built underneath, I stare up at the stained-glass windows and the sculpted statues, and I try to remember who I was last Christmas. As Omar plays with his boot's laces, the priest reads a prayer, bombastically filling the air with proclamations. I'm not really here for advice. Some people pick up Bibles to read along, but I don't bother. Everyone has a reason to be here and not somewhere else on Christmas Eve. I'm not interested in the service, only the room and the opportunity to be among others.

A year ago on this day, I was a widow with no husband to bury. I spent this evening with a napkin in my hand, sitting in one of his sisters' homes, invited out of pity and expected to mourn Halim openly. I wore a beautiful sequined evergreen dress, dark like a Christmas tree, offset with black stockings from the knee down. I glittered in old jewelry borrowed from family. Everyone was dressed up for the meal, even the children, and almost fifty people passed through the apartment that night. As currents of relatives, neighbors, and family acquaintances filled their plates, I sat in an armchair off to the side of the buffet table with a portrait of Halim behind me, mascara running down my cheeks behind darkly tinted sunglasses, stoically feeling trapped.

A year ago, I would never have admitted to anyone that I loathed Halim's family. He loathed them too. We simply acted our way through it. No one says those things out loud in Lebanon. Tayeb, I'll say it now because no one can stop me here, thousands of kilometers away. His family is fascist! Phalangists. Mercedes-driving, France-idolizing, swimming-pool-in-the-mountains, horse-grooming colonial elites who think themselves better than everyone else, except those few who live in luxury along the Mediterranean Rivieras. But before Halim was kidnapped, they were rarely in our daily lives. Halim was one person with me, another with his family. He wore different faces, as the occasion called for them. I did too. Beirut is a mask society; you never show your true feelings, only those feelings others expect to see.

Which is why I spent last Christmas weeping in front of his portrait at his sister's home. With Halim gone but not officially buried, I was in limbo. I could never remarry. I struggled to contain my emotions, which made me unpredictable. They had a responsibility to provide for Omar, who unlike me was their blood. But the obligation to me was beginning to strain their patience.

I remember my brother-in law Abu Hazzen coming to my armchair beside the buffet table, kneeling before me as other family members stole glances from across the room and, in an orchestrated flourish, holding back tears as he kissed my hand. He reached toward the portrait of Halim behind me.

"Ya Muna, ten thousand tears for your losses." He stood up and, still holding my hand, said, "Come, let's go somewhere more private so we can talk."

He led me back through the kitchen, where the Ethiopian help diligently prepared more plates of food to be sent out. Fascists like the Khourys always keep African help locked away in their homes, their passports withheld until their contracts are complete. We went out to the back balcony that overlooked the parking lot below. From where we stood, we could see generator lights on in almost every apartment as far as the eye could see. Through his bushy gray moustache, Abu Hazzen lit a Dunhill cigarette and said, "I've been told that, within the month, Halim's application for immigration to Canada will be accepted."

"What?" I said. All that paperwork hadn't entered my mind in two years. "I thought that was forgotten."

"These things are never forgotten," he said. "They just take a long time. We made some calls and the file ended up in the right hands."

"Tayeb, what do you want me to do? I can't go to Canada and live on my own. What do I know about Canada?"

"I think you should reconsider."

"You do."

"You're young. There's nothing for you here."

"What does that mean, *nothing for me here*?" I hissed, unable to control my emotions.

"This is what we can offer." He drew an envelope from his breast pocket. "We will arrange your passports and help you with the travel arrangements. And this ten thousand American dollars will be our gift to help you get started on your new life. After that, we have nothing left to offer. The monthly allowance has to end. But this is all in the distant future, and you'll have a long time to prepare. Six months. By August, my father has plans for your apartment."

"You can't make me leave my home when I have nothing left," I said.

"You were already leaving. Halim filled out applications."

"You're pushing them through against my wishes."

"We're pushing nothing through. You're a French teacher. The immigration agent says that moves you into the top tier of desirable candidates. You'll find work quickly. As for your family, your father has already accepted his gift for the holidays."

Abu Hazzen tapped the envelope, which was already in my hands. We both knew I had no choice, and I wasn't surprised by my father taking money like that, as it was his nature.

"You're making me leave so you can erase your obligations." I had fresh tears streaming down my face by then.

"We're helping you leave so you can forget yours. Give yourself and your son a new life."

Sitting in this foreign church, clutching Omar's hand, I remember clearly what I said next: "You're sending us to our deaths."

A year later, I don't believe that anymore. A year later, I pity the woman who sat at the end of buffet tables and mourned to soothe her in-laws' consciences at her father's beckoning so they wouldn't cut off her allowance. Those last two and a half years in Beirut, Halim wasn't allowed to die, and I hadn't been allowed to live. Without Halim there, the Khourys felt they were forced to take me in, provide. And I was beginning to see how exhausting it was to have them in our lives, a never-ending performance of silent gestures and indignations.

The sermon comes to an end. I haven't really been listening, but I've enjoyed the sounds it makes.

"Yallah, habibi, let's go light a candle." I don't say it's for his baba, even though it is. I find I never mention Baba anymore. I'm waiting to see if he brings him up, or if he remembers. Ever since the night of his fever, I've listened to him sleep every night, for any other sign that he remembers, but it hasn't happened again. I don't want him thinking about Halim tonight if he can help it, because he genuinely seems calmed by the sounds of the church. I've told him Santa will only leave a present under the tree if he sits quietly and behaves. "In an apartment this small, you can't be here when Santa makes his delivery. He'll just skip us. We have to go." So he has incentive to be good. He's not like me, flailing like an octopus tangled in the fishing net of bad memories. He just wants a used toy.

Lighting candles is fun when you're young. I remember when I went to church with my parents, lighting candles was my favorite part.

"Tayeb, you choose," I say to Omar as we stand before the cup of candles. He surveys them for the longest one he can find. Trembling, he holds the wick to a flame. We watch it smoke and quickly catch.

"What do I do next?" he asks.

"You don't remember? Yaneh, you make a wish or think of someone special."

Omar holds the candle for a while, probably thinking of the most effective wish he can imagine, and then he finds a stand in which to place the candle. Who did he think about, I wonder, but I'm too afraid to ask.

"Now can we go open my present?" he says.

I smile and nod. "Let's go."

We tie up our scarves, pull down our toques, slide on our thick gloves, and step outside into the frozen evening air. There's no wind tonight, and our breath hangs in clouds under the streetlights. The stores have closed, and all the last-minute shoppers have gone home to extravagant family dinners. I wonder who here gets to play the youngest daughter, the indignant sister-in-law, the wife in mourning, the unfortunate cousin? I miss such nights and feel relieved to be free from them all at once.

We walk back up University, turn onto our street, and enter our building. The TV in the office has been turned off, and even Mr. Saltzman has gone home for the night. Omar impatiently presses the elevator button the whole time it takes to arrive, while I caution him that doing so could only slow it down. In the apartment, the tree we assembled stands by the television. The only plant in the apartment, I realize now as I look around.

I've wrapped the game of Monopoly using news-paper, and as he waited for me in the hall before we left, I quickly slipped it under the tree. Without taking off his coat, he runs to it, picks it up with excitement, and tears the paper off.

"What is it?" he asks, unsure if he likes it or not.

"It's a game. Tayeb, from the commercials."

"On yeah, Monopoly. How do you play?"

"How do you play?" I repeat, more asking myself than him. "You can play many ways. I think you use the pieces to build a city."

"Wow!"

"Right?"

He opens the box, pulls out the board, and begins to plot neighborhoods with the green and red buildings. "Look, there's a silver dog," he says.

"And a fast car. You can do anything you like with this. It's pretty fantastic."

"It is," he says.

As he plays on the kitchen table, I make myself a tea and turn on the TV. Ronald Reagan is giving a speech at a podium. An image of missiles being fired in Iran fol-lows. Here, I rarely see any updates from back home on the news. Yaneh, no one here cares that it's still going on. Lebanon's war is an old war now, about to celebrate its first decade. Unless it reaches new heights of horror, there's nothing new to add. Maybe I shouldn't think about it so much either, I decide as I sip my tea. Omar lets out a squeal as he uses the carved horse to plow through a row of houses and they tumble onto the ground. Maybe a horse is just a horse. I wonder if he feels anything different in its weight anymore. If he remembers who made it or why it's here. He never lets on. Maybe too many other changes have happened and now that past is gone. Maybe next year will be better. Inshallah.

HERE THE NIGHTS ARE ENDLESS

On New Year's Eve I hear shouts and laughter coming from apartments in the building where some students are having parties. A car honks in celebration as it drives past. 1987. On TV, newscasts show fireworks from cities across the world. Whether it's next door or in Melbourne, Australia, it all feels so far away.

After two weeks of only ever leaving the apartment to buy food or walk Omar when it wasn't too cold, I am relieved to be going back to work. Tayeb, after paying the weekly rent I have exactly fourteen dollars to make it to the end of the week, and I've run out of activities to entertain a boy who doesn't know what to do with himself.

It's a new year, and I don't know what to do with myself either. I'm eager for a change, for anything to break my way. As I turn the shower tap off and step out from under the water's heat and look into the steamed mirror, I whisper to the only person who will listen to my complaints. "1986 was the year I failed to become who I thought I could be. This year I'll become someone else."

"No matter who you become," Halim says back to me, "I'll still know who you are."

I hate that he says this. I hate how mean it sounds and how its truth resonates. Maybe I hate what I'm becoming. In a small fit of rebellion, I open the bathroom door to let the steam siphon out and take Halim with it. I'm alone again. This year, I'm letting go of my ambition to stand in front of a classroom. It hurts too much to keep trying to break into a world that was dangled before me but never actually available.

"It's 1987, and I might as well just be a weight-loss consultant," I say to myself in the mirror now that the steam has cleared. A hotline operator, a phone-order taker, a shipper of boxes, an ear whose only purpose in life is to swallow the sadness of strangers.

I look directly into my eyes as I say this, leaving nowhere to look away. I need to hear this truth.

The following Monday, when I walk into the Nutri-Fort offices for the first time this year, I find a notice on the bulletin board: Lise Carbonneau has called a meeting for all the sales representatives.

"We're launching a new campaign today," Lise announces after a few remarks about how perfect her holidays were. "It's the biggest campaign of our annual cycle. It's called New Year's Resolution."

She raises her hand and clicks the clicker, the slide projector whirs to reveal an ad of a young woman, attractive in tight-fitting workout wear, her lustrous blonde hair in a loose bun. She's busy, engaged, modern. She looks as if she's been crossing things off her to-do list, her skin glistening ever so slightly to give the impression that she's active. She stands at her kitchen counter, a carefully plated portion of the Chicken Parmesan (Box 23) before her. Behind her stands a man, maybe her husband, maybe her boyfriend, his hands around her waist, as if noticing her again for the first time in years.

"Look at how her gaze communicates inner fulfillment," says Lise. "Look how happy they look. This is our demographic ideal. This is who our clients want to be. And that's the point, isn't it? This could be you. That could be your perfect man, if only." She laughs, and a few other women in the room laugh along with her. Yaneh, even I chuckle. "If you don't have a problem, don't wait until one appears. And if you do feel like you have a problem, don't wait any longer."

The big red tagline confirms this: *Now's the time*, it reads, as if glossy magazine paper can transform into an old and trusted friend doling out the advice you need to hear. Underneath, *50% off your first three months*. Then, *We take care of your meals. You take care of you.*

"That toll-free hotline number puts prospective clients through to you," Lise informs us. "This ad is an investment in your paycheck. What happens in these next two months sets the tone for the rest of your year. Let's see who can perform."

Lise clicks, the projector whirs, and a slide appears that lists the publications the ad's been placed in across Québec for the months of January and February. *Chatelaine, Marie Claire, La Presse, Elle, Flare, Redbook, Good Housekeeping, Cosmopolitan*, some other ones I don't recognize. "Yours truly had a hand in those placements," she says, taking a little bow.

We clap gently.

"People see this ad, and they say to themselves, *I can do it*. It's easy. We give them a number: ten, fifteen, twenty pounds. We tell them to attack it mathematically. We've all had holidays. We all have love handles, double chins. Who here is not guilty of eating too much cake? Good for you, I say. You had fun for a few weeks. You fell off the wagon and had seconds at dessert or dipped your little pinky into the gravy bowl while doing the dishes. But now's the time to tackle those extra pounds, or they'll snowball."

You take care of you. I mull it over as Lise articulates a series of self-improvement strategies we can use on the phone. *The time is now.* Yaneh, I can do that, I convince myself before the presentation ends. Lise is so convincing. She speaks in warm, approachable gestures, like an expert. She cites studies as if she's memorized and tested all their findings. She has an encyclopedic knowledge of the weight-loss marketplace. She dresses as if her closet is one of the fashion magazines she leaves behind for us in the lunchroom as if to tell us, *Follow my lead and fix yourselves up.* I still can't believe she has children, a five-year-old and a twelve-year-old, girls. She stays late at the office every evening and must spend at least an hour preparing herself every morning. Where does she find the time?

I walk back to my desk to prepare for the first call. I sit down and, for the first time this year, take a long look at the food boxes standing there before me as they have the whole time I've been here, and I ask them: Have you changed me, or have I changed? I look around the room and see that none of the women who started the same week as me is here anymore. After nearly two months I'm pretty senior. I'm either good at what I do or the most desperate of them all.

The first call comes in. I pick up the receiver and press the blinking red button to put the caller through.

"Merci d'avoir appelé Nutri-Fort. Mona à l'appareil. How may I help you?"

"Bonjour, Mona, I'm calling about the ad in this Saturday's *La Presse*."

"Oh good, it caught your attention. Is it something that's been on your mind?"

"Mais oui. Most of my adult life, you could say. How does this work?"

"Well, the basics of it are quite simple really. A person gains weight because they eat too many calories for their body type. But it can be so confusing keeping track of where those calories come from. Nutri-Fort's food packages are designed so that you know exactly how many calories are involved. We take the math part of dieting and make it transparent for you to see. We talk about the food you're eating and how to put together combinations that work for your lifestyle. It's about building new habits. Along the way, you can think of me as your helping hand."

"That all sounds great. Is it expensive?"

"Not when you start at fifty percent off for the first three months. Quite a few clients have reached their goal by the end of that period. We have a strong success rate. Those who do continue with us find that it's worth it for them to have some guidance. We have an introductory package that we send out to each new member that explains what you can expect and what's happened with others like you. I'm sure you'll agree, the weight can be isolating. You shy away from many activities that others wouldn't give a second thought. This program is about giving you a community so you're not alone."

"Is it discreet? I don't want the whole world to know."

"I completely understand. You pick up the packages like groceries, at one of our many pick-up locations. We're in most malls. The food arrives in an unlabeled cardboard box, so it looks just like any other package someone would pick up from a store or post office. The bill to your credit card appears as our company's initials, so if anyone happens to see your monthly bill, it won't be obvious. As for the food packages, they're there for your information only. The food itself is easy enough to remove and put on a plate or in Tupperware if you're eating with others or taking it to work or somewhere public."

"But … does it taste good?"

"We don't want to compromise the best part of eating! The plan works around portion sizes. There's a little less added salt and sugar in each offering, but most clients find they adjust to that pretty quickly."

"Okay, that all sounds great. So how do we start?"

"Well, let's start with your name. Who am I speaking to?"

It continues like this all day. Yaneh, over the next six hours I field eleven inbound calls from the ad campaign, and I sign up all of them. Lise is right: with the discount introductory offer, it's never been so easy to make that commission.

It's not until later in the week that I finally have some time to call back my existing clients. Sylvie Leduc in Brossard is first on my list. She's been on my mind ever since we last spoke in early December. Her husband was an issue, I've written in my notes, and her story stayed with me. I try not to think of my clients, and in most cases that's not a problem at all. But there are a few among them who pull me into the theater of their lives as soon as they answer the phone.

"Bonjour, Sylvie, it's Mona from Nutri-Fort. Am I catching you at an okay time?"

I hear her turning down the TV in the background.

"Yes, yes, Mona, I'm just having my afternoon coffee."

"Happy New Year. Did you have a good holiday?"

"Yes, it was nice," Sylvie says. Is that indecision I hear flowing in her voice? She sounds like she wants to talk but doesn't know where to begin. It's up to me to ask the right combination of questions.

"I find it's a bit boring now that it's all over," I say, with a little laugh.

"I like getting back to normal," Sylvie says. "It's such a spectacle, every year."

"Have you stepped on the scale since the New Year?"

"Mm-hmm."

"And?"

"Two thirty-six." The brightness in her voice spills over into sadness.

"Listen, it's okay. You have to forgive yourself the slips during the holidays," I say. "We talked about this, remember? The holidays are a special time. It's okay to take a break for a bit."

"Twelve pounds is a lot," Sylvie says, sounding as if she's wiping a tear from her eye. "All I can think is how long it took me to lose it. It's just so hard sometimes."

I have to think carefully about what I'm going to say as soon as I hear the client become emotional. If I misjudge my next words, Sylvie will step back and push me away. "I understand your disappointment. It's too bad that we can't always live up to the standards we assign for ourselves. But we can all do with a little forgiveness when we look in the mirror."

"I can't even look at myself in the mirror anymore." Sylvie is sobbing now. "Do you want to know how my holidays went, Mona? Can I tell you something I haven't told anyone else?"

"Mais oui, Sylvie. Everything we discuss here is confidential."

"Do you know what my husband told me over the holidays? He said he was cheating on me. Again. He said *again*! This whole time, I had no idea. He said the first time had been a mistake, but this time it wasn't. I just smiled at him, I was so shocked at what I was hearing. It was Christmas Day and his parents, his brother and his family had all just left our house after I'd slaved over a big turkey dinner for them, the boys were off in their rooms, and he was sitting at the kitchen table with another scotch in his hands as I was collecting all the plates and glasses from around the house, you know, getting everything over to the sink so he could watch me do his fucking dishes while he told me I wasn't good enough for him to even tell me I'm not good enough. He got upset at me, for listening like that, for saying nothing at all and scrubbing a plate, as if my not responding to him confirmed I was dumb, and so he said he'd been acting his way through our marriage. He said he couldn't act anymore. He said he was ready to tell me now because he was convinced it was my fault. He says I did it to myself. I felt so humiliated."

"This is horrible news, Sylvie. I cannot begin to imagine what you must be feeling right now."

"I wouldn't wish it on you for anything, Mona."

"Go on, have a good cry. I'll listen. It must be such a relief to say something, to let it out."

"You know what irritates me the most," she says, crying openly now. "That bastard doesn't deserve my secrecy."

"He doesn't deserve you, Sylvie."

"I just feel so trapped by it all. Where do I go from here? Do I break up my family? Do I lose this house? I love this house! I don't want to even imagine what this will do to the boys. They're learning to hate all women because of him."

"You're strong, Sylvie. You're the foundation of your home. It goes wherever you are. Don't give up on your boys. You have a bond with them that he can never replicate, and they will always respond to your love. As for your husband, he's lost his way. There is something inside him that's broken and instead of fixing it, he'd rather look across the table and blame you."

"He said I do nothing for him anymore. He doesn't recognize the girl he fell in love with."

"You gave him two children, a home, a center from which he could stray. He doesn't know what he's losing. Mark my words, Sylvie, it is you who will come out of this the stronger person."

"I'm glad someone thinks so."

"I really do," I say. Ya rabi, it's always so hard in these moments to back away and remind myself that I'm not a friend but a phone consultant. My job is to find a way back to the weight-loss program without losing her. To keep Sylvie on track so that at least one ambition in her life remains stable for the moment. "Think of your diet plan as the first step to making him see that you are better than him. That he's the one who's lost his way."

This time, it doesn't work. She's no longer paying me any attention. I listen to her weep and I do my best to console her, and then we make plans to speak again in a few weeks.

After the call ends, I genuinely don't know how I'll find the strength to return to this telephone for my next client. I look at the receiver in its cradle with genuine fear. The intensity of calls like Sylvie's causes me to lose sleep. I can't see the purpose in what I'm doing. I can't help; I can only listen and offer a few words, then mail some boxes.

People's lives here are easier and harder all at once. They're never at risk, but their safety and stability can turn into a cage. They're free to pursue their dreams, but they're held back by the responsibilities that come along with them. I hear it in all their complaints: schedules, kids, spouses, work, extended family. And they begin to gain the weight. Then there's an ad in a newspaper or magazine to contemplate, maybe bookmark or tear out, and someone to talk to if you muster the courage to pick up the phone and call. But the big joke at the end of it all is that the person you'll talk to is me, someone you would never talk to in a million years. Ya rabi!

Omar's teacher has asked to meet with me. The morning of the meeting, I wake up before dawn to the sound of my radio alarm: a station on the AM dial that plays classical music. I sit up in my sofa bed and yawn. Outside it's snowing again, and the mesh of the window screen is frozen solid with icy clusters. I put on coffee, go wake Omar, and then begin to get ready for the day. Because of the meeting, I'll be going into the office a bit later.

As we eat breakfast, I ask Omar, "What's his name again?"

"Monsieur Pierre."

"Ya rabi, tell me, don't lie. Are you in trouble?"

"I don't think so."

"No fights, no bad grades?"

He can't think of anything. When I ask if his teacher is meeting with other parents too, he shrugs. I give up, take his almost-finished cereal bowl over to the sink, and instruct him to go brush his teeth.

I haven't seen the inside of his school since I came here last August to enroll him. At the time, I was naïve enough to worry that I might end up teaching at the same school as Omar. I wondered how he might react to *me* being his teacher. I had no idea what was to come. Now, as we're walking through the halls past lockers and class-room doors and art projects pinned to the walls, I once again feel the ache of not being a teacher. I thought I could let it go like one of the New Year's resolutions I learned about at work, but simply saying I'm going to let a thing go doesn't magically make it happen.

We arrive at the door to his class, and I see his teacher's name – Pierre Gagnon – and then *classe d'accueil,* which is the classroom all the immigrants are assigned to until they learn enough French to join the kids in the regular classes.

I tap firmly.

"Entrez," I hear M. Pierre call.

We step in, and Omar's teacher rises from his desk. He is a thin man with a thick mustache and wire-rim glasses, balding but with long hair that's tied back in a braid. Unlike the more formal look I usually saw on male teachers back home, he wears sandals with thick wool socks, a loose vest, and a beaded necklace.

"Welcome, Madame Heddad, comment ça va? What a pleasure to finally meet you." He reaches out to shake my hand. Then he turns to Omar and says, "Bon matin, mon grand. Would you mind giving your maman and me a few minutes to talk? Go play with your friends."

Omar gives me a helpless look that I instantly read as *but I have no friends.* Smiling, I nod to the door as if to say, *See you later, habibi.* Once the door closes behind him, M. Pierre pulls two of the kids' little chairs out and invites me to sit with him, our knees jutting up between us.

"Thank you for taking the time to come down here."

"Of course. You have a nice classroom."

On the wall above the board there is a large blue-and-white Québécois flag, as well as a series of posters labeled NOUVELLE-FRANCE that show European explorers planting flags on mountains and navigating rivers.

"I try to make learning a living activity," he says. "I want to surround the kids with history and culture so they learn it for themselves. I'm sorry, I'm talking very fast. Do you understand me okay?"

"Yes, sure. I speak fluently. I am a French teacher too."

"Ah, that's wonderful. I didn't know that. Where do you teach?"

"I'm not teaching anymore. It was before we moved."

"When did you move here?"

"Last August."

"Oh well, bienvenue!" He lets out a laugh and slaps his thigh with his hairy hand. "It's hard to get any information out of Omar."

"He doesn't participate?"

M. Pierre shakes his head. "I try to engage him. But most of the time he just stares out the window and waits for the day to end. Is he tired? Does he stay up too late?"

"No, I make sure he gets to bed at eight every night. He generally sleeps okay. I don't know if he's told you, but before we moved to Canada, he missed school for a year. In Lebanon, where we come from, there is war."

"He hasn't told me anything," he says, looking surprised to be hearing what he's hearing. "I think he's afraid of me. What does his father do?"

"His father died three years ago," I say, trying to keep it casual like it's something to be taken lightly.

"I'm sorry to hear that." He turns serious. "I think Omar is having a hard time with your transition. As you can imagine, I see a lot of immigrant children passing through here, a lot of lives changing, a lot of feelings, many languages. Some kids' stories are so sad."

"I suppose you think Omar is one of them," I say. "I've been trying to shield him from it all, but I see it's not working."

"What I can do for them is teach them enough French and socialization skills – you know, how things are here – to help them find how they fit in."

"How should they fit in?"

"Well, in Omar's case, it's how to concentrate, to be present, to communicate. I've seen him for three months, and all the other kids in our group have made advances in that time."

"He's not used to going to school in French, or going to school at all."

"Maybe he missed too much. I wonder if he shouldn't stay in the third grade next year."

"It's already been hard for him. I had this talk with your directeur, Monsieur …"

"Beaupré."

"Yes, Monsieur Beaupré, and I don't want him to feel any more alienated from school than he already does."

"I understand your position. Omar has to do something, make some effort to communicate. I can't let him just coast through without meeting certain standards."

"I'll have a talk with him. I just want you to know, it's been a major adjustment for him. We're still finding a balance to our lives. Maybe I work too much, but I don't have a choice at the moment."

"Is he getting enough attention at home?"

"What's that supposed to mean?"

"You said it's just you and him, Madame Heddad. You said you work too much. Is he spending too much time alone? Is he being ignored? I'm beginning to see how it might be hard for him to integrate if he sits at home all day alone."

Yaneh, is he concerned or is he accusing me, I wonder, feeling uncomfortable and more than a little ridiculous in the small chair. He watches me with the intent eyes of a police investigator. "He's here with you. This is where he should be integrating. With all due respect, it's your job too."

"Madame Heddad, I don't want to argue with you. And I see you're getting upset. My point is, I've been teaching here for almost thirty years, and no matter what else is going on at home or in the world, the problem never gets resolved until everyone begins to try harder."

"Try harder at what exactly?"

"Integration."

"Last year was very hard. The most difficult. This year I'm hoping will be better. Don't push him down any further than he already is."

"If I can be honest, it's you who must take a greater interest in his education and in participating in our society. I understand if you miss home and its ways, but oftentimes in my experience, immigrants need to work harder when it comes to absorbing our values and our language."

"It's funny, I thought I was coming in here to talk about a bad assignment, negotiate with you over a test question."

"How can Omar integrate, how can he improve his French, if the only time he speaks it is here? He'll just sit at his desk quietly and wait for class to be over so he can go back to speaking Arabic as soon as he leaves. Then what will he learn?"

"Must he trade one language for the other?"

"Madame Heddad, when was the last time you communicated with anyone here in Arabic? Do the Africans speak Arabic?"

"Well, some of them, I think …"

"Do the Vietnamese speak Arabic? Or the Polish, or the Portuguese? He's not going to need it. What Omar will need is better French than he currently has. Listen, Madame Heddad, I see that you're young and that being a single mom is hard. I'm just trying to help you out. Make it easier on him. Try harder to speak French at home and give him a chance to fit in. We have just under six months left to see if we can turn things around. It's plenty of time. That's why I wanted to talk to you now."

The school bell rings.

"D'accord, Monsieur Gagnon," I say, standing up. "Thank you for your time. I'll talk to Omar."

As I walk out of the school, I see all the kids lining up with their class ready to file in. I wave to Omar, who's in the back of one of the lines not talking to anyone, and blow him a kiss. "See you this evening, ya habibi," I wave.

He ignores me as a few kids around him laugh among

themselves. I realize I shouldn't have spoken to him in Arabic here, and that if M. Pierre were standing behind us, he'd probably judge me some more. I raise the hood of my coat against the wind and hurry down the street to work, even though it's the hardest thing to leave him at that school all alone now that I know it's so miserable for him. Yaneh, I blame myself for turning a blind eye to his circumstances and telling myself he's fine while I try to build us some kind of life.

In the evening when I come home, set down my bag, take off my coat and join him in front of the television, I pull him toward me and hold him in my arms like I used to do when he was little, in a way he doesn't always let me do anymore. But I don't care: he's my child, and he's suffering an invisible pain, and I've taken advantage of its invisibility. I kiss the top of his head.

"Keefak? How was school?"

"Okay."

"I met with your teacher."

"And?"

"He says you don't participate. Is it true?"

"We're not learning anything. It's embarrassing to be in that class. The rest of the school makes fun of us."

"Habibi, you don't like it there, I know."

"I'm sorry."

"Don't be sorry. I know it's not fun to do the things we have to do. But can you try for me, just for a couple more months? We have to get you out of that class, but the only way to get you past that teacher is for you to pay attention and participate. Talk to your teacher, make a friend."

"Okay, I'll try," he says, more to make me happy than anything else.

"Shukran, ya albeh." I kiss the top of his head again to let him know the talk is over and he's not in trouble. "Now what do you want to have for dinner?"

"Hot dogs?"

"Yaneh why not?" I say. "It's Thursday. *ALF* is on. Yallah, go wash up and get into your jammies, and we'll watch it and eat dinner."

I fuss over him as he gets off the couch and goes to his room. I find fresh pajamas in the laundry basket and smell his hair to tell him to shampoo. Once he's in the bathroom and I hear the shower run, I dig into the freezer and pull out a Box 14 Hot Dog Dinner Set that I have left over from before the holidays. We sit on the couch and eat them with ketchup and nothing else, because he says that's how they taste best, and on TV that silly doll dances around the living room as an exasperated dad puts down his newspaper. What's ALF getting up to now? ALF disappears into a closet and returns with a red wig that supposedly belongs to the dad. The show's audience laughs, and so do we. I lean over and kiss Omar's head one more time, just so he doesn't forget that he's not all alone.

Tayeb at least I'm getting paid today. Tired from another five days of busy phones, I can't wait for this week to end. I line up at three o'clock on Friday afternoon with all the other salespeople, and I wait for my turn to get my check from Lise Carbonneau.

"Heddad, Muna," Lise says, rifling through the envelopes. "Ah yes, the famous Mona." She gives me a smile as she hands me the envelope. "Good work. Enjoy."

I smile at her. Up to now I wasn't even aware she knew who I was. I sit in meetings, I pay attention, I follow her phone philosophy, I keep to myself and do as I'm told because I can't afford to lose this job I don't want. It's not complicated. But her recognition, that catches me by surprise.

Back at my desk I open the envelope and find that the number typed on the paper is larger than I expected, more than double my previous paycheck. It accounts for the phone calls since we came back to work two weeks ago, when the New Year's Resolution campaign began. I can't see any other explanation for it. "Mabrouk, ya Muna," I congratulate myself under my breath as, in my head, I jump up and down on my desk. My commission has gone up because of all the calls and new memberships I filed. This concept of commission, to be honest, was unclear to me at first. I didn't get very much of it before because I was following up with clients already in the blue folder, which adds only a few extra dollars, fifty at most. But now I'm signing up my own clients. I've brought in more new clients these past two weeks than in all the weeks I worked before the holidays.

I sit there and I stare at the check. Two desks over, a fax machine is chirping and spitting paper into a tray. The fluorescent-white office light is threatening to burn that salty tear of joy into the creases around my eyes. The corners of my eyeballs are starting to sting from looking at the check too long. It's not only a number on a piece of paper. It's also good news. Which, tayeb, I generally don't expect anymore, what with all the rejections I got during my teaching interviews last year. Add in Lise's compliment, and that makes for two pieces of good news. Maybe I'll cry if I think about how lucky I am for too long. No. I would never allow anyone in this office to see me cry. No one here knows anything about me, not how I live and not where I come from, not even that I have a kid. As soon as I leave the office in the evening, I disappear into thin air, and I don't reappear until I pass the receptionist on the way in next morning.

"Au revoir." I nod and smile to the new receptionist on my way out. "Have a good weekend."

"Bonne soirée, Muna," she smiles back. Even the receptionist has changed over since I first started. To her, I'm a veteran.

I've left a little early so I can go to the bank to deposit my check before the numbers on it magically change back to what they once were, like Cinderella's pumpkin. I remember reading that fairy tale to Omar when we slept in the cellars in Beirut. Someone had found the French book in one of the storage rooms, and over the months it got passed around from one family to another. The ones who couldn't read French were happy to just turn the pages and look at the pictures. I would read to him and translate it to Arabic as we lay back on the mattress, a flashlight beam between us lighting the pages. Teenagers and toddlers alike, all the children, fell in love with Cinderella as the story traveled around the storage units, from one bedtime story to the next. She was a hero to us; we were living in our cellars just as she languished in her attic. I feel like all this money in my purse is going to disappear at midnight, too good to be true.

Am I floating on air? I look down, and my little feet in their heavy boots are barely touching the sidewalk's icy asphalt. Outside, it's already dark. It's always dark now, toujours. It's gloomy when I leave our building in the morning, and it's threatening when I come back in the evening. I haven't felt sun on my face yet in 1987, though I can see it sometimes out our windows at work throughout the day. It's not a long walk up University Street, but it is icy, and I have slipped a few times before while rushing. Yaneh, it hurt for days. The trick, I've decided, is to look for dry patches ahead of each step. It takes longer, and so I make it home later than usual, but tonight I'm not going to feel guilty about that. My purse is full.

"How are you today?" I say to Omar, kissing him on the top of his head. "How was school?"

"Okay," he says, not looking away from the screen.

"Did your teacher talk to you?"

"Ai."

"And, what did he say?"

"He gave me extra homework."

"Did you do it?"

"Not yet …"

I pick up the remote and turn off the TV. He sighs.

"Then let's do it now. I'll make dinner and we can talk through it at the same time."

I change out of my work clothes in the side of his bedroom where I keep all the laundry, and by the time I return to the kitchen to prepare supper, Halim's wooden horse has been pushed to the side of the table where Omar has his yellow Duo-Tang open.

"So, what do you have to do?" I ask, rifling through the fridge to drum up an idea for dinner.

"I have to answer these questions in a special exercise book he gave us."

I look over the assignment before him, its title *Life in Quebec*. Tayeb, okay, M. Pierre, I roll my eyes.

"Yallah, read me the first question."

He places his finger under the words and studies them intently before starting. "Why is it important to speak French in Québec?"

"Yaneh, what does your teacher think?"

"I don't know. Maybe to be understood?"

"That sounds like something he'd say. Just tell him what he wants to hear."

That seems to make sense to Omar. Relieved of the

responsibility of thinking for himself, he starts writing what he thinks M. Pierre would say if he were in the room. This goes on for five questions about the language, values, and history that they appear to be learning at school.

After dinner, I leaf through the workbook to see what else it contains. There's a section on Samuel de Champlain and Jacques Cartier, whose names I already know from the bridges south of the city that I can see from the Nutri-Fort windows. There's a section on the Catholic Church and one on Nouvelle-France and another on the Quiet Revolution. I find it mildly interesting because I have no way of knowing this information from my work or from watching TV. It's useful to have a better idea of how people think.

After I put Omar to bed, I turn on the TV and set it to a low volume so I can watch the screen without really paying attention. My mind is on my paycheck. It will happen again next time, I scheme at the kitchen table. Absentmindedly turning over the wooden horse in my hands, I think about how I could make even more. I already have more phone calls booked to pitch prospective customers than I did last week. At the start of this week I couldn't see how I would make it through another five days, and now I'm looking forward to Monday morning.

There's an old movie on CFCF-12. It's another one of those mysteries with the detective named Columbo, who looks like he shops at the Vêtements 2000 but who turns out to be very good at his job. I've seen several of his TV movies before. He has a way of working into a case by letting people underestimate him. People underestimate me too. This is what I love most about television in Canada: if you leave it on all the time and forget about it, it will become another voice in your head telling you what to think about yourself.

Ya Allah there are moments when I want tenderness, warmth, another's breathing beside me as I sleep. Tonight, after my shower, in the fog of all that steam crowded into the tiny bathroom, I take Halim by the hand, and I smile in a way that beckons *you can't say no*, and I whisper, "Yallah, come to bed," and then I open the door, and as all the steam flushes out into the hall and disappears, I dash the five steps into my open sofa bed and bury us both under the pile of old duvets. I disappear under the blankets. In a ball, my body sags the sofa bed in the middle. Why would my head dare look out on this last night of January, as the wind outside rages against the windows with its pellets of ice and the temperature drops down to minus thirty-six degrees?

"This is my mistake," I say, nuzzling into the bristles along Halim's cheek. "I shouldn't have fallen in love with you all those years ago in the mountains. Kfar Mechki was a village built on our desires. Nothing there was real."

"Love creates too many wants."

"It's dangerous to want so much."

I don't want much anymore. Just a touch of that fantasy I once had when I was seventeen. I've made it through this first month of 1987 with my desires eaten down to the whiteness of their bones. I am barely a skeleton of what I once wanted. Only through starving myself of these urges can I begin to see the ghosts of my life as friends, as confidants. Be stoic, I say to myself. Want nothing. Exist only in the service of others. Breathe new life into memories. Reverse-engineer absence. Smallah, I can make Halim. I can make him kiss my forehead. But if I close my eyes and try to kiss his neck, I'll kiss only the lumpy corner of my pillow. In the eternal darkness of winter, I fall asleep this way to calm my anxiety, a wet pillow between my lips.

The next morning, I get out of bed and start all over again. I put on coffee, I wake up Omar, we brush our teeth, I comb his hair, he picks the lint from my sweater, I pull his hand out the door, we kiss in front of the school, and then I stagger down the street against a wall of wind, and I don't look up until I'm safely into the underground city. I shiver, shake off my coat, swear. I walk past movie posters for upcoming screenings at theaters whose marquees I've passed downtown – the Imperial or Loew's or Cinéma de Paris – lit up in bright lights at eight in the morning like they're ready for a Hollywood premiere. I know about these things because I sometimes watch *Entertainment Tonight* while making dinner to practice my English and also because I'm curious about famous people, especially movie stars. I've always loved movies, even before I was able to watch them in bed.

I loved going to the movies as a girl. It was one of the only places my father took me regularly, long after my older brothers and sisters had moved out. We had one movie house in Ashrafieh, Le Palais des Rêves, run by an old Maronite who had once acted in a bunch of Lebanese and Egyptian films and used his earnings to build the theater. I know this because he was a friend of my father's and they would chat for a while every time we went. He always insisted we go in for free, and maybe that's why my father took me there in the first place.

Each week a new film would play. Back then maybe once or twice a year we would get one of the big Hollywood films, a years-old reel that had already run its course on projectors across Europe and had finally been sold from Italy, Greece, or Turkey, the very edges of Europe's distribution market, into the Arab world. When I was older, I usually went to the matinée with my girlfriends, the first screening of the day, when Le Palais des Rêves played older beach films from France, lonesome seaside towns with Brigitte Bardot, the ritzy boulevards of Monaco with Louis de Funès, the cliffs of Monte Carlo with Jean-Paul Belmondo. Watching those movies is how I fell in love with the French language and decided to become a French teacher.

For the two evening screenings, the films mostly came from Egypt, where all the most beautiful Lebanese actors went to become stars. I love Omar Khorshid, who acted as well as he sang and played guitar before he died in a car accident a few years ago. Everyone in the theater knew a Rahbani family score when they heard it. Yaneh, Fairouz, who was also a Heddad, was married to a Rahbani.

They say Fairouz and I are related. Fairouz is Lebanon's darling, like that Ginette Reno is to the audiences of the French talk shows here. Great-grandparents on her father's and my mother's side settled in our village after fleeing Constantinople by way of Cairo. Or something like that. All our dreams lead back to Kfar Mechki.

By the time I get to the office and sit at my desk, I'm feeling that much warmer to have even a little bit of Fairouz's blood coursing through my thin hands. If only Fairouz could know how far her blood has traveled. I will sit down and write you a letter, ya Fairouz, I say to myself as I open the blue binder. Even though she toured the world many times and a plane ride to Montreal means nothing to her.

It's a funny thought to have, *inutile* as Lise Carbonneau would say. Fairouz and I are third cousins at best. The connection is a family joke, brought up by the drunk uncles at outdoor dinner tables to accompany the arak and pistachios. I miss those large family gatherings in the mountains of Kfar Mechki on summer nights! The pebbles beneath my feet, the shadows cast by candles, the cedar trees framing our courtyard, the feral cats ambling along the rooftops hunting birds, the cooking that began after breakfast and involved all the women on the street, many of whom just dropped in to gossip and have a coffee, or to bring over an extra pan of knafeh they'd just happened to make. I was unmarried then. There was no war. Everyone was welcome. Children ran in and out. The old men would play backgammon and speculate about which branch of Fairouz's family related back to them and curse out politicians and movie stars alike for a laugh. Old men who would say anything to get you to laugh. Old men who spent lifetimes perfecting a punch line. Now that they're gone, I think their jokes were perfect.

With the snow outside the office windows pushing me further inward, it's easy to forget there's anyone around me. The office darkens beyond the edges of my desk. I am both here and not here, an actor, a ghost. I pick up the receiver, take a deep breath, and dial my first number of the morning. "Bonjour, ma chérie. Oui, c'est Mona de Nutri-Fort à l'appareil. How are you?"

One Saturday in February, on the kind of clear-skied, almost zero-degree, bright weekend morning I haven't seen all winter, the phone rings as we're about to head out to do our groceries for the week. It catches me by surprise because our phone hasn't rung much since I stopped applying for jobs. My first thought is that one of the jobs I applied to last fall is calling me back with predictably bad news. But then I remember what day it is and think, no, it's just a wrong number. I set down my purse, and with my coat still on, I clear my throat and walk back to answer the phone.

"Bonjour?"

"Can I speak to Omar please?" It's a child on the other end.

"May I ask who's calling?"

"Chang, from school."

"Oh, okay. Just one moment."

I turn around and look at Omar waiting by the door after I've spent the past half hour pushing him to get dressed, pulling on his snow pants, finding his mitts, and I think, *Ya rabi, we're going to have to do it all over again*. I point the receiver at him and say, "It's for you."

He perks up. "Who?"

"A friend. I didn't catch his name."

He pulls off his mitts and runs to the phone. I try not to listen, to give him his space, because anyone can see that this is a big moment for him, the first time he's ever received a phone call from another child. He's not saying much, just grunting a *oui* and a *non* now and then. I made him memorize our phone number when he began coming home alone. But mostly I'm surprised that, without saying anything, he's taken my advice and made a friend. He's becoming secretive, this child; he's off living his own life. I'm happy and concerned for him all at once.

Finally, he presses the receiver into his snowsuit and turns to me. "Mama, can I go play at Chang's house today?"

"Where does he live?"

"Here, he says talk to his mom." Omar points the receiver at me.

"Allô?" I say into the receiver. I exchange pleasantries with the woman on the other end, whose French is not that good, and then ask Omar to find me a pen so I can write down the address and metro station. "Okay, see you then," I say. "À bientôt."

"Can I go?" Omar asks before I even hang up the receiver.

"Sure, habibi. I just have to figure out how to get there."

We walk down University Street to the nearest metro station, where I know I'll be able to find a city transit map to study.

Along the way, I say, "You've made a friend. That's great. Why didn't you tell me?"

He shrugs.

"Well, good for you. Didn't we say it's good to try to make friends? What's he like?"

"He's in my class. We sit at the same table. He's not really my friend. I just told him my phone number."

"Well, maybe he wants to be your friend. It has to start somewhere. Are you excited?" I ask, a bit jealous.

"Maybe," he says, looking at me like he's trying to gauge what answer I want to hear.

We push through the metal doors at the base of a skyscraper and walk down to the metro level to where the map hangs on the wall.

"Okay then. Help me find Chinatown."

Our fingers follow the green line from McGill, where we are, a few stops over. It's not far at all. I look at the address and see that the street we're looking for is only a few blocks south of the station. "It's nice out," I say, not wanting to spend the money on four metro fares. "Why don't we walk there?"

We go back up to street level and walk along Sainte-Catherine Street to Saint-Laurent. I rarely ever walk through downtown on weekdays anymore because of the cold and because the sidewalks are usually crowded with office workers and students, but on a sunny Saturday morning such as this one, we have them practically to ourselves. It's early still, and in this part of the city there's signs of the fun people had the night before: cigarette butts outside strip club doorways, empty bottles lying on their sides in the alley beside the Spectrum concert hall, discarded ticket stubs outside the movie houses. We walk south along Saint-Laurent and discover the big red gates of Chinatown. Behind the main streets lined with open vegetable markets and closed restaurants, we find the rows of small duplexes and triplexes where Omar's friend lives.

We arrive at a door that matches the number I've written down, on a second-floor landing of a triplex.

"Yallah, ring the bell," I say.

Omar presses the lit-up button and we wait. Soon the door opens.

A boy Omar's height stands there. When neither of them says anything, I prod Omar. "Aren't you going to introduce me to your friend?"

"This is Chang. Chang this is my mom."

The boy holds out his hand. "Ah, you're using your French," I remark to Omar. "That's good."

Chang's mother shows up, drying her hands with a dishcloth. "Bonjour," she says, smiling widely.

Chang says something to his mother in their language, and she appears to agree. He turns to me and asks, "Can we go play in my room?"

Both boys look up at me expectantly.

"Sure, go."

They run down the hall and disappear.

"Come in," Chang's mother waves.

"Ah merci, but you're probably busy."

"I'm not busy. Come in, sit. Coffee? It's so cold outside."

"Okay." I say, taking off my boots. Tayeb, the groceries can wait a few hours. I'm also curious what other apartments look like in the city. I can't sleep on a sofa bed in a place filled with other people's furniture forever. So as she walks me through her home, I'm noticing how it's bigger than ours, with higher ceilings, better lighting, wider rooms and a hall to separate one half of the apartment from the other.

"What a nice home you have," I say.

"Merci. Sit, please. Coffee, tea?"

I ask for tea. It's less inconvenient to prepare. "I'm Muna, by the way. Thank you for inviting Omar over. He's new at school. It's been hard for him to make friends."

"My name is Su-Lin. Everyone calls me Winnie," she says, placing a kettle on the stove and preparing two mugs. "We are new too. Chang says the school is bad. It's not easy to make friends. I tell him, If you like someone, ask for a phone number. Don't be shy."

"Have you met Monsieur Pierre?"

"The Buddhist monk." She laughs and I laugh too. It's true that his sandals and long, baggy shirts make him look a little eccentric.

Bringing over a tray of tea and biscuits, Winnie begins to tell me about her life. She works as a housekeeper at the Queen Elizabeth, one of the big downtown hotels on Dorchester Boulevard, just a few minutes from the Nutri-Fort office. It's the only job she could find where she doesn't have to speak to anyone, and where she can be finished by three p.m., in time for Chang to come from school. She has a husband she hardly ever sees. He owns a dépanneur down the street, near rue Saint-Denis, where he works from seven in the morning to eleven every night, seven days a week. Her older son helps out on the week-ends. "He's there now," she points with her right hand at the wall. "You work?"

I nod. "It's not a very good job," I feel the need to qual-ify immediately after, "but it will have to do until I find something else."

As efficiently as I can, I explain my situation with ap-plying everywhere to be a French teacher without any luck. "They say I have to go to school again and get a degree from here."

"I am an accountant," Winnie says. "But here, I need to take a course for a special certificate. It's very expensive. Now, I do accounting only for the dépanneur."

"I wish someone had told me before," I find myself complaining. "I mean, you must know. It costs a lot of money to immigrate; there are so many fees you have to pay. Along the way, all anyone does is promise us there are so many jobs that need to be filled by people with our skills. But then we get here, and no one wants to give us those jobs."

I've said too much. I don't even know this woman, and here I am complaining.

"It's very hard," Winnie agrees. "We bought the store, but now the building has problems with foundation, the roof leaks water from snow. It's all expensive to fix! People steal from the store. One man, we caught him stealing, and he hit my husband. We called the police. The police come, do nothing, and later an inspector from the Régie comes to give my husband a ticket for having signs in Cantonese for Chinese foods!"

The boys are making a lot of noise, banging some toy against the floor, and Winnie takes a moment to yell something in their language into the other room. I shout too: "Omar, wa'af hal dajeh!"

That quiets things down.

"Your husband works?" Winnie asks a moment later.

"It's just the two of us." I try to say it casually again, but it never works. Then I realize she may assume I'm divorced, which I have learned from the Nutri-Fort phone lines is something that happens a lot here. It's unheard of where I come from. I sense that Winnie doesn't know how to respond either, and so I add, "It's okay. It's been a few years since he died. I don't think Omar even remembers him much anymore."

"Your French is good!" Winnie says, shifting the conversation.

I'm relieved to be changing the subject. "Merci," I smile.

"You are a French teacher?"

"Oh, I want to be. As I said before, I tried. But I can't afford to go back to school now. There's no time. It's too late for me."

Winnie laughs, apparently taking that as a joke.

"You can teach me. My French is bad! I need a teacher. I can pay you."

"You're not serious," I smile. "There are free French courses you can take from the government. Why pay me?"

"Classes are not at a good time, and they are too far. I work all day, and I am here with boys at night. I need help. But I must improve before the accounting certificate course. Maybe you can help me please. I insist to pay you."

"Really, you're serious. When?"

"Weekends. The boys can play. I can make nice coffee and snacks. You teach me French, and I pay you ten dollars an hour."

"Oh please, I feel embarrassed taking your money. From the mother of my son's new friend, no less."

"I don't know teachers," Winnie says, exasperated. "I need help."

I've never considered private tutoring before because I wouldn't know how to get started. But why not, I think to myself as she stares at me pleadingly. I can gain some local teaching experience. Omar can gain a friend. And we would have something to do together on the weekends.

"Okay," I say. "If you have no other option, then let's give it a try. Do you want to work on writing, reading, conversation, or all?"

"Everything. I am bad! You like Chinese food? I'll make some for you."

Before I can refuse, Winnie has run into the kitchen and returned with a plate. A second later, I'm trying not to look rude as I bite into a doughy, steamed pork-filled bun and Winnie describes what she will make for next Saturday.

T' fadal, it may have been almost bearable to be outside on Saturday when we walked to Chinatown and back, but right now, just a few days later, an Arctic wind is whipping Montreal like it's decided to finally kill us all. On the streets between the office towers, everyone I pass covers every part of their body except for the barest slits across their eyes.

I haven't inhaled fresh air in days. At the apartment, we breathe through the building's humming ventilation system and with it the crisp warmth of old steam pipes and the aromas of cooking and whatever wafts over from the garbage chute down the hall. Whenever I scamper down the sidewalk from Omar's school to the underground city, my face is wrapped in someone else's old scarf; I suffocate behind someone else's stresses and secrets. I unveil myself only once I'm underground, in the borrowed, recycled air shared by the web of metro lines and office towers. At my desk, I inhale the electrified dry air of the office, with its particles of carpet dust and disinfectant.

I pick up the phone to make a call. It's time to check in with Louis Laflamme. As I search the file for his Hydro-

Québec extension number, I wonder if he's developing feelings for me. In our talks since the new year, I have been very careful not to lead him into any more talk of cutting himself, and he hasn't brought it up again. But I've sensed that he might be misinterpreting my tone, and imagining other motivations in our phone calls. He's left a few messages, once during the holidays, and twice after office hours since then. He'd make some comments about the boxes he was enjoying, noted one he didn't enjoy. Then he just kept on talking, and even though he continued to speak in a friendly manner, I had trouble following what he was talking about. I must admit, the last time I didn't listen to the end of the message. It was too long.

I played that one back for Lise, to get her advice on what to do. She said, "Ignore it. In my experience the few men who call in get attached and start to think there's something between them and us that isn't there. This is why we don't use our real names, and you only ever use the office phones to call clients."

Louis makes me feel a little uncomfortable, but mostly I feel sad for him. I understand how that attachment can happen over time. How a person can hear affection in the inflections of my voice articulating his feelings, feel intimacy in my advice as he wrestles his demons. He speaks a bit longingly, wanting validation, reciprocation that I can only offer to a point. Most of my other clients know where that line is, but some can't help crossing it. The risk of it being there thrills them. They want to see how far they can go. These clients have to be gently pushed back to where they belong, with delicacy and deflection.

The phone rings twice, and then he picks up.

"Hydro Québec, department des comptes. Monsieur Laflamme à l'appareil."

"Bonjour, Monsieur Laflamme. It's Mona, your nutritionist, how are you this morning?"

"Ah, Mona, comment vas-tu? Give me a moment to close the door."

I hear him stand up, a door closing, then when he picks up the receiver again I say, "I'm well, Louis. And you?"

"Oh you know, up and down, down and up."

"Did you pick up the last order?"

"Yes. Merci."

"Good. And how are your numbers for this week?"

"Okay."

"Are we up or down? It's okay either way."

"Up."

"Why do you think that is?"

On the other end, I can hear him choke up a little as he thinks about how to best say what he has to say.

"I've been having these pains," he finally says.

"What kind of pains?"

"In my back. I went to see a doctor about it a few days ago."

"I'm sure it's nothing, Louis. You sound worried. Are you worried?"

"I am a little worried."

"What did the doctor say?"

"He took some blood and said his office would call if there was anything to discuss."

"So he wants you to go on with your everyday life."

"Mona, you know me now, so I can say this. My everyday life is not so good. And then when you add physical pain, ben … it all becomes unbearable."

"I understand, Louis. It must be very difficult."

"I have trouble sleeping because I worry so much. And then I have trouble getting up because of the pain in the morning."

"At least we have the plan to provide you with some structure and certainty as you navigate this troubling time. We all face challenges, Louis. This is why we build routines into our lives, to offer us a path to follow when we can't think clearly."

"I really look forward to your calls, Mona. Every time we have a call scheduled, I sit in my office and wait for the phone to ring. The rest of the time I just think about your advice. I know I've been weak a few times, I called and left you messages. You were right not to answer."

"Thank you, Louis. The truth is I'm there with you all the time. I am in the menus you eat and the schedule we make. The people in our lives can be there for us even when they're not, you understand? But sometimes if you try to grab onto them too strongly, they just disappear."

"You're so right, Mona."

"So tell me where these extra calories are coming from."

"From the casse-croûte near my apartment."

"Why do you still go there, Louis? One of those meals is the equivalent of four of the boxes on your plan."

"The waitress is friendly. We chat. The cook knows me by name. I like the feeling of eating with other people around. The conversation when they're not busy. You know, the hardest part about this program is eating alone. Do you know what it's like to eat alone all the time?"

"It's difficult. I understand."

"You probably have a husband, children. A woman like you probably has it all. What do you know about loneliness?"

I bite my tongue. I don't want to share anything about my personal life with this man. All I can do is wince at how he's trying to provoke me into doing that. "That's not fair, Louis," I say.

I've taken too long to respond, and he senses I am upset.

"I'm so sorry, Mona. I'm really not myself today. I don't know why I said that. I really don't mean it. I would never want to hurt you."

"It's not helpful to think of me as someone who can be hurt or protected, Louis. I'm just here to help you. *You* have a goal in your life. *You* want to make a change, to find some happiness to replace what's been making you feel bad for so long. All I want is for you to succeed."

"You're my lifeline, ma chère Mona."

I let that one pass. I just want to get to the end of this call without causing any harm. "Tell you what, Louis, why don't we make a compromise. Stick to the plan for dinner, then go to the casse-croûte for a coffee or a tea. Sit at the counter. Talk to your friends, the waitress and the cook. Keep that part from your life if it makes you happy. Keep what makes you feel good and let go of what isn't good for you. That diner food is not helping that pain you feel inside, I guarantee you."

He seems to like that idea. For the rest of the call we focus on the various menu combinations he can try. After we hang up, all I can think is *Ya rabi, I'm glad that's over*. I breathe a sigh of relief and look out the window. Sixteen minutes and twelve seconds. I write down the time in the log, with a note about the client's complaint of pain, visit to the doctor, and general worsening depression. Staring out at the falling snow, I wonder if the program isn't for Louis. If he should be seeking out some other form of help. It's not my place to say that to him; all I can do is keep him on the program for as long as possible.

"Tell them whatever they need to hear," Lise advised during one of her presentations, "and never push them too hard. We offer one kind of solution, but the people we get are sometimes looking for another. Better they reach out to us than to another firm."

The whir of office activity begins to seep back into my head: sales reps on calls, inventory statistics coming in on the fax machine, a few people chatting in the kitchen, a pair of delivery men diligently carrying off boxes upon boxes of old paperwork to be archived. Nutri-Fort is doing better than I could've ever imagined such a business doing. In Lebanon, even though women are obsessed with how they look, no one ever talks about weight loss, much less builds a business around it. Who can have such an idea without reliable phone lines? Yaneh, I know the whole approach must mean something to the clients because they keep ordering the boxes. But it only works so long as they can imagine Mona, without me getting in the way.

Now that I have a little extra money, what do you want me to do? Of course I'm spending my lunch breaks shopping. I'm avoiding this brutal winter at all costs by not venturing above ground any more than I have to. Ya Allah, other than shopping, there's nothing else to do in the underground city but sit in a food court and ignore the eyes of people who want your table.

It started with a pair of gold-plated earrings at Ardene (less than five dollars!) after my first big check, and now every week I get paid, I've begun to prowl for clothes or little luxuries to remind myself that I'm still young and that useless trinkets can make me feel good too. I talk about it like a secret, but it's my money, and anyway, there's no one to keep a secret from.

Today jewelry or clothes won't do. I want a bigger thrill. I want to test my limits for pleasure. I'm browsing new VCRs at the RadioShack. I hear many good things about these machines, mostly from Omar over dinner. All he knows about them is that Chang has one and he gets to go to the video store and rent movies and then make popcorn, turn off the lights, and watch new movies on the couch.

"We have movies on TV," I say.

"You can watch VCR movies anytime you want," Omar insists. "And they're more fun to watch without commercials."

"But what if you need to go to the bathroom?" I say, playing the devil's advocate just to keep the conversation going.

"You can press pause," he says, as if I should know that. "You can stop the movie in place, and then when you're ready to start watching it again, you press play, and it picks up right where you left off. You can also rewind and fast-forward too."

Smallah, pause. What a feature. I walk back to where the units are displayed. A VCR is the one thing I haven't been able to find in the building's storage room; they're simply too new and coveted. But the winter is so long and we spend so much time indoors. I'm reasoning with myself, looking at the lowest-priced one in particular. There's a video store here in the underground city, near Peel metro. I walked in to look around one day, out of boredom, and fell in love with all the movie posters on the boxes. It made me realize just how much comes in boxes here, from food to films. There were so many of them. There was even an entire science-fiction section, which doesn't interest me at all. But Omar would like it, seeing movies I've never heard of, with actors I never idolized. And a VCR comes with us when we move. I can see myself as an old lady using this machine. It's a good investment.

For the first time since arriving in Canada, I'm making enough money to breathe. I can count on it coming in. Over the first three weeks of Saturday French lessons for Winnie, two other women have also joined in, each one with her own ten-dollar bill. They're both from Winnie's church. Winnie told them about our lessons, and they immediately asked if I had room for others. It turns out they can't go to the government language classes in the evenings either. They've gone before, but the teacher is condescending and makes no effort to figure out what conversation skills they need, focusing too much on verbs and reading literature about how to be a model citizen. But with me, they say, they can bring plates of food, and I can guide them through conversation scenarios as all the kids run around us, making noise. It's an imposition on Winnie, and I don't understand the food, but I've started looking forward to the sessions every Saturday.

I can relax around these women, even if we don't understand each other very well. There's a distance between how we see the world, and it forces us to speak slower to each other, to really think about and listen to everything we say. They're learning a language, but I'm learning something too. I see how we all live together in the shadows of this city. People on the street see women like us and expect that after moving here, we'll carry on for the rest of our lives as housewives, ignorant, doting mothers to assimilated schoolchildren. No one pays women like us any attention. We're harmless, inconsequential. We're allowed to go on with whatever life we can piece together, so long as we don't get in anyone else's way. But ya rabi, things are so expensive here that not one woman I've met can even afford to think like that.

And with that, I decide I can't buy the VCR. Life is still too unpredictable to spend that money right now. I've talked myself down, and I feel a little sadder for it.

I turn around and say to the store clerk, "I'll be back next week maybe." My lunch break is over and who wants to carry a big box like that through the office for everyone to see?

"Bon après-midi," he says, not looking away from the TV section where he's watching a game show across six screens at once.

I take an escalator upstairs and walk through echoing marble-and-tile corridors back to my office. I find a note on my desk from Lise Carbonneau. *Come see me when you're back from lunch. Merci!*

Lise Carbonneau has never called me into her office before. What could she want, I wonder, trying to recall if there's anything I could've done wrong. Things have been going so well, but I can't be sure it won't all end, just like that. Maybe Louis called to complain that I wasn't giving him the kind of attention he was paying for. A shudder goes down my spine as I walk to her door. I knock.

"Entrez," Lise calls out.

I step into her office just as she steps off her Stair-Master. She points a finger up at me as if telling me to pause like a VCR, and she finishes up a call on her headset while I take a moment to admire the exercise machine. After talking myself out of a VCR, having one of these in the office seems like a completely different level of opulence. I try to imagine one by my desk, but I know I wouldn't have the confidence to exercise at work, or at all.

"Sit, please," she gestures, removing her headset. She sets her elbows on the large desk, leans in, and smiles. "Muna, right? Am I pronouncing that correctly? I never know."

"Sure."

"Great. Do you know why I've called you in here, ma chérie?"

I shake my head. I'm trying to decide if she's genuinely being friendly or if it's all part of some psychological game designed to make my bad news feel worse once she drops it on me. I can't afford to lose this job. I should be ready to tell her that.

She picks up a file on her desk and opens it. "Muna Heddad, I'm happy to report that you've broken a Nutri-Fort record."

"I have?"

"You've sold more diet plans in one month than anyone else at this branch."

"Oh, that's good," I say. "I didn't know I sold that much."

"Can you believe you sold more boxes than the next three sales reps combined?"

"Not really."

"Muna," Lise says, "I think you're like me."

"Please," I blush, "that's not possible."

"We're cut from the same cloth. You have a talent for this. Everyone who does well on the phones has something special about them. With you, if I'm honest, I think they like your accent. Your sound and your mannerisms. It's almost as if ... as if talking to you doesn't count."

"Thank you," I say. "I try to tell them what I would want someone to say to me."

"You understand the formula. It's natural for you to be completely outside their lives. They feel like they're talking to someone on the other side of the planet. It makes them comfortable enough to share the real reasons for their weight gain. Deep inside, they all know when and where and why it began to happen."

"It's hard to look inside yourself for truth."

"It's so true. See, you even make me feel comfortable. There's just something about you, Muna."

"I just listen to them. It's normal for me."

"It's a talent what you do, a real skill."

"Thank you."

"Congratulations. By the way, the top seller every month gets a two-hundred dollar bonus. You'll see it on your next check. For now, you can walk back out onto that sales floor with your head held high. You're our biggest earner this month. I think you could be a real asset here."

"Thank you, Ms. Carbonneau."

"Lise."

"Merci, Lise. I'll continue to work hard."

I shake her hand, unable to look her directly in the eye because I might cry at her kindness, I turn around, and I go back to my desk to make my next call.

Being on the phone after that meeting feels different. I'm friendlier, I have more energy in my voice, I believe in people again. Tayeb, it makes a big difference when a woman you admire congratulates you and says you have talent. Before today, I've never thought of myself as a person with a talent. Everyone likes Mona, especially Lise. I suppose I have a talent for inventing people.

I look to Lise Carbonneau's office door and think how lucky she is to be Lise Carbonneau! Attractive, confident, athletic, capable of turning on a switch deep inside a person just by gracing them with a few well-chosen words. If I thought it possible to love another woman, then it would be Lise. I know that she must look around the office and see an interminable river of failed phone artists coursing through. I've overheard the reps she's had to pull into her office and console behind closed doors when they burst into tears at the cruelty of a client who's suddenly decided the trip wire between decorum and intrusion has been crossed. I've witnessed her Monday-morning realization that another dejected operator has disappeared over the weekend. Lise must be under a lot of stress. I'm pleased to be recognized for alleviating it, or at least not adding to it.

After work, I head back down to the underground city to inspect the VCR one more time before the shops close. With the news I have now, I look at the machines' prices and lists of features with new intensity. *I'm going to do it*, Mona is whispering in one ear. *Do it*, I hear Lise whisper in the other. I can feel it in my skin.

"Have a change of heart?" says the sales clerk who saw me earlier. "It's a great model. Did you know you could program this to record your favorite TV shows when you're not home?"

"I did not know that," I say. "But it is expensive."

"If it's a deal you're after," the clerk smiles, "then I have just the thing for you."

I follow him down the aisle toward the clearance section, enjoying the fact that someone is trying to sell *me* something for a change. Ya Allah, nothing makes me feel more alive than being pursued like a prize.

I'm in the shower, but really I'm on a big stage, standing in front of a microphone with a tambourine in hand. I'm my third cousin, Fairouz, Lebanon's darling, and all my old uncles are sitting in the front row explaining how they're related to the most magnetic Arabic voice in the world, but I don't need the rationale in this moment because *I am Fairouz*, and my eyes are shut tight against the hot stream of water beating against my eyelids, and I'm singing through the rain, and everyone seated behind my uncles in the sold-out theater is clapping along to the drumbeat of the darbouka, the swell of the orchestral strings, and my song. I have been singing to them for more than twenty minutes. I'm leaving everything I have to offer at their feet. As I climb the final crescendo of this lovelorn ballad of ache and haunting, I raise my tambourine in the air and shake the orchestra behind me to a standstill. I love that moment in between the very end of the song and the split second after when the audience realizes they can applaud. I savor that moment in the shower. And then it hits me: the waves of applause rolling in, swaying me with their adulation. They keep applauding me for a long time, until I finally turn off the water.

In a white cloud of steam, I step out of the shower and look into the mirror as I dry off. "They all love me," I say, "but what about you. Did you ever think of me as a prize? Did you ever pursue me?"

"I tried," Halim says, with a little laugh. "But who knows what I was doing. I wasn't very experienced at that …"

Without letting him finish his thought, I grab him by the hand and, naked, run out of the bathroom to huddle deep in the dip of the sofa bed's mattress, a pocket really, a cupped hand of stuffed cotton and weak springs. It's past midnight, and I feel alive. From under the pile of duvets, I can see flashes of TV light streak across the window, where snow is not falling but speeding past, as if my apartment is the perfectly still, perfectly balanced center of a tornado. Yaneh, I am like Dorothy in *The Wizard of Oz*, that movie often on TV after midnight. Only I have no clothes on. I'm too warm and I want company.

"Tell me the story of the first time you saw me," I whisper as I twist under the covers, alive and restless.

"Do you remember the Café Younes, the only café in Kfar Mechki? It was so hot in the afternoons that summer, even in the mountains, and the air swirled with dust clouds as everything around us turned to sand. It was as if we were in an hourglass. I saw you there, you were seated off in the corner with your legs crossed and an open book on the table in front of you."

"What were you doing?"

"I remember I was on the sidewalk outside, on my cousin's motorcycle, waiting for a friend. I looked in and there you were, in the corner, hiding in the shade, trying to keep yourself invisible, lost in some thought no one else could know and yet suddenly the center of all I was looking at."

"Was I beautiful?"

"In your way, you were. There was something in your pose, the way you looked out at nothing, that made it clear, as soon as I laid eyes on you, that you were not someone who would hang around in the background or turn into a passing distraction, that you would be the center of my life from that point on."

"Wa'ef, ya hayete," I coo. "You're just saying whatever comes to your lips. Everyone knows you came looking for me at Café Younes because my friends had told you I spent hot afternoons there, reading books, surrounded by the tables of old men and their worry beads."

"Mazbout, I wasn't there to meet a friend but to find you. And I was scared to be chasing after you. Once I arrived at the café and stood outside on the sidewalk, beyond the shade of the covered terrace, with its little round tables and foldout chairs, I froze. As mopeds parked behind me and a car honked and a cat scurried past with fresh trash in its jaws, I was paralyzed by you, kint khayef."

"Afraid of me? What did you see?"

"I saw you. I saw the way your neck curved up to your ear, how your hands folded across the surface of your book absentmindedly, holding the page. I saw your lipstick's glistening imprint along the rim of your white teacup. I saw things in you that I'd never really looked at before in anyone else, and I understood that it was me who had to change, who wasn't up to the moment, that I was maybe too young and a little too cocksure for my own good and that I'd had blinders on my whole life."

"I was special to you?"

"In a way that no one else could ever be."

"You're a silly man just standing there. Come in out of the sun and talk to me already."

"Marhaba, Muna. Keefik?"

"Good, ya habibi, I feel good. Yallah, sit down."

"Can I get you anything?"

"I already have a tea in front of me, remember?"

"It's disarming sitting across from a person I've only just seen for the first time, to see the texture of your skin, to follow the rhythm of your breathing. I'm imagining reaching across the table and running my fingers through your hair."

"Smallah, do it."

"I wouldn't dare, would I? There are so many people around. You have your world and I have mine. We don't share a world just yet."

"Do it. In front of all these people. I dare you."

"I still remember how thick your curls felt in my fingers, like they were holding my hand."

"And my cheek?"

"I worried you'd feel the clamminess of my palm against your skin. I was genuinely nervous."

"That's sweet of you. You know I was waiting for you. My friend said a boy would come looking for me."

"I knew that we would walk out of there together, and I felt lucky to have been coaxed into this dance with you. Would you like to dance?"

"Now? Here? Between all these tables, in this mountain village high above Beirut, where no one knows that we're falling in love?"

"Come, take my hand."

"What are we dancing to? I know. Fairouz."

"Her voice is mesmerizing. She's your cousin, isn't she?"

"We're a family of talents."

"How I miss the feel of your arms around my waist and your hands on my back."

"I miss this music, the stages, the orchestras, the poetry, the expressions of love, the drama. Nobody makes music like that here."

"Do you remember how we danced like this at our wedding? I took your right hand in mine, cradled the small of your back, and we glided across the room like two birds on a current."

"Is that what love is, you think, two birds on a current?"

"I think so. An electric caress, a tenderness, a pull when you feel unwanted, a push when you feel in doubt, applause from a dark room."

"Then what?"

"I think I said something along the lines of 'You look like no one else I know,' and you said, 'Is that good or bad,' and I said …"

"Good, you said good."

"And I broke out into this smile that was at once pride and embarrassment, and you said, 'That's only because you don't pay attention,' and I had to admit that was true, and I said, 'I won't ever do that again,' to which you said …"

"Don't lie to me."

"I was nervous. I wasn't thinking ahead to a time when I would become distracted, when I would look to the streets for hours to figure out the best time to get gas for the car or worry about keeping Omar alive. I didn't think of it as lying. I just didn't have any sense of what would come later."

"Please don't worry, ya albeh. I'm just teasing."

"I live with the regret of every single thing I promised you. We made plans together. Now you're living them alone."

"You're still here with me. I feel you always."

"I do what I can."

"I know you do."

The music comes to an end and the other customers of Café Younes quietly pull their tables and chairs back into place as we sit back down.

"We came in here separately, but now we're going to leave together," I say.

"Let's go then," he says. "I can't wait."

We get up and I steal glances at him as he pays our bill, jokes with the waiter. We walk out onto the sidewalk just as the morning is ending and the sidewalks are starting to get busy with the lunch crowd threading in between cars.

"Can I walk with you?" he asks.

"I'm not going far," I say.

"I have nowhere to go."

Just then, a bomb explodes farther down the street, and for a moment the deafening blow silences everything but a car alarm as the entire neighborhood cowers in anticipation of what will happen next. As we stand up again, a drizzle of dust falls down upon us like snow and turns our bodies white from head to toe. Halim takes off his shirt and wraps it around his face.

"Don't leave," I say.

"I'll be right back."

He leans down and, through the fabric, kisses my dusty lips. I close my eyes and hold the kiss for as long as I can. When I wake up again it's morning, the sky outside is blue, but the pillowcase near my mouth is still damp from our embrace.

I stand in front of the mirror, and for the first time since I started working at Nutri-Fort, I ask myself, *Ya Allah, Muna, are you gaining weight?* I turn to look from the side, straightening my back and raising my blouse to better see my stomach. When I hold my breath, maybe I can pretend nothing's there, but in reality it's only so long before I have to breathe and it bloats back like a sponge under my belly button. As I do up the brown slacks I brought with me from Beirut, they feel less forgiving than before. Ya rabi, even my underwear feels tight!

It's true what clients say on the phone: one day the fat just appears out of nowhere, and after that it becomes impossible not to see it there. All my life, I've been bony like a marionette. I never developed the curves other women got. I have no breasts, and my hips look like the sharp ends of a shopping cart. But here it is, fat bulging and flaunting, protesting for my attention. I disdain it for showing up now of all times, just as I'm beginning to feel hope and gain a foothold in this city. It's goading me into buying new clothes when I've just spent all my money on a VCR. *Yaneh you'll fit in these clothes whether you like it or not!*

I say to my uncooperative figure in the mirror. I resolve to eat only the boxes, starting this afternoon. Although I can't say no to all that cooking I must eat at Winnie's home, which is where I suspect this belly was conceived. I've been eating everything I'm handed to avoid insulting these women who think I'm useful. I walk to get my coat, clenching my stomach muscles.

"Omar, yallah, let's go," I say, "or we'll be late."

Today, we take the metro to avoid the cold on our way to the weekly French class. The underground city will only get us so far before we have to face the wind. The group is meeting at eleven for an hour-long lesson plan for writing and reading, and then we'll all stay for a lunch and coffee that gives everyone the opportunity to socialize while practicing their conversational French with me there to correct them. It's twice as long, but they've all asked for more social time and they're willing to pay for the extra hour. There are now six women crowded in the living room and four kids playing in the bedroom, and sometimes when the kids all come in to help their mothers with spelling games, I end up with a group that's almost the size of a regular class. When that happens, and I can see all their eyes resting on my lips as I enunciate slowly, for the first time since coming here I feel like a real teacher, doing what I'm meant to do.

When we arrive, the apartment already smells of pans frying mushrooms and peppers and root vegetables I've never used in my cooking before, back when I used to have time to cook. These women use soy sauce in everything, like I use olive oil. The six of them are taking turns in the kitchen, each with a different dish on the go. When I step into the room, they all turn and say, "Bonjour, Madame Muna."

"Hello, everyone," I say. "Smells delicious."

I don't know everyone's name yet, especially the two new ladies steaming bok choy and making rice who are joining us for the first time this week. At Winnie's instruction, a special pot of tea is brewed for me and brought to my usual place at an armchair in the living room.

For some of them, their French is nonexistent, but they're highly motivated. Winnie tells me they all met through their church. They are trained as doctors, dentists, lawyers, accountants, but they're all having problems breaking through the language and experience requirements put in front of such professions here. And no one has found an optimal teacher yet. Québécois teachers grow impatient with their pronunciation and break down at the lack of common words they share, turning condescending with pictures of cats and buses. The Cantonese ones understand them too well, and the familiarity means no one tries as hard. I'm not Québécois or Cantonese, and that's what they say they need: patience without the possibility of cheating.

We sit in a loose circle around the living room, notepads and pens in hand. I've devised lessons to suit them. Using a portable chalkboard from the Salvation Army, I write down and pronounce a series of phrases that will be useful to them. Each week, we focus on a different social situation: clearing a check at the bank when dealing with a suspicious teller who asks too many questions, talking on the phone to a government official in order to navigate the endless bureaucracy needed to get anything done, asking questions on public transit, and so on. With parent-teacher conferences coming up, today's lesson focuses on scenarios for that meeting:

How is my child's writing/reading/math?
My child does not understand the homework.
Does he/she get along with the other children?
Can you recommend a book we can use to practice
at home?

We work with these cues and see where the conversation can go, making sure they have the words to get there. Inevitably, we will all be lectured on our children's weakness in French, how if we don't speak French in the home with our children, they will never improve to the level of those who are born here. The ladies discuss what they want to say, and in the end we agree on three sentences:

We must speak our native language at home or else
it will be forgotten.
We practice, but it is not the same as talking with a
native French speaker.
Is there extra homework you can provide to make
up for this grade?

In all honesty, it doesn't matter what we say back. After chatting with these ladies, I see that most of the teachers they encounter are like M. Pierre. They get into teaching out of a strong belief that they need to defend the French language on behalf of a people who want their own nation. People like us are a burden to that cause. A generation ago, these teachers didn't even want immigrants in their schools. But now the government believes all newcomers must learn French and participate in the goal of independence. Our kids have to try harder, the teachers always complain. Otherwise it's a life of failure, stuck in an underworld of relying on other immigrants for jobs, working in the back rooms of restaurants and hotels and warehouses. Throughout the lesson, I can hear the children in the bedroom yelling at each other in French, even though they have a common language. They adapt, but they don't imitate. Why should they?

The women write down these phrases, and we sound them out together. I play the role of the teachers in the meeting, and we run through some practice conversations. Each woman takes a turn. They laugh knowingly at the questions I ask or pause to question how they can better navigate a particularly sensitive juncture, bringing together phrases from previous lessons to fill in the dialogue.

To finish, I have them each read an entry aloud from a dog-eared, six-volume children's encyclopedia I've picked up at The Word, a used bookstore near my apartment, taking the time to work through pronunciations and meanings, which I note on the board. They all copy down what I write.

When the lesson ends, the ladies put away their notepads and call in the children, whose job it is to lay out plates, napkins, water glasses and, for Omar and me, cutlery. They all use chopsticks with ease; they can bend their fingers into any shape and confidently move food from the bowls into their mouths. But the only time we tried it, we made a mess and everyone had a good laugh.

Yaneh I feel so honored by the respect they afford me, the extra time they invest in making me feel welcome. I'm never treated that way, and I've forgotten that I deserve it just like everyone else. Over lunch, they talk about their lives to each other, in French, and I listen and I pause the conversation, just like the VCR, if we need to take a moment to talk about what's being said and how best to say it. I don't know what they're talking about a lot of the time. I'm not part of a community like them. I prefer to be on my own. I need a clean break from my Lebanese life and what it's done to me.

We finish eating an hour later, and all the women discreetly set their twenty-dollar bills on a tray in the hall as they gather their children and get ready to head back home. I don't want to make them uncomfortable when they're doing this, so I insist on washing my teacup, and hunched over the sink, I keep my hands and eyes busy.

As I'm folding up the dishcloth, Winnie comes in and says, "Next week, we have more students. Good news. More money for you."

"Ya Winnie, shukran," I say, taking her by the hand. "For everything. The food was delicious. You are an angel. But we can't impose on your home like this. Look how crowded it is in here. It would be impossible to teach anyone anything if we did that."

Winnie looks around her living room. "I have a solution," she says finally. "We can use the church basement. It's much bigger."

"Smallah." I find myself more at ease speaking my own words around the ladies. They freely throw around Cantonese expressions that I've learned just by paying attention to their repetition and context.

"Much bigger," Winnie says. "Enough for a class for fifteen, twenty students."

"Do you think there's that much interest?"

"Even more."

"Ya rabi, I would have to start a business," I say.

"If you start business, I be your accountant."

"I *will* be your accountant," I say gently.

"I can do good work for you." Winnie smiles. "You *will* pay me very well."

I've never seen anything like it. Even though the snow-banks around the neighborhood are still piled as high as my shoulder on some corners, the sky turns black as ink one afternoon and it begins to rain. At the office, we all sit up and look out the windows as large drops slap against the glass like palms banging on a door. What could this be? It turns to a beating as I file my afternoon reports. By the time I'm ready to head home for the day, the radio is calling for a big ice storm. I'm trying to understand it, because I've never seen weather act this way. I could never dream up weather this powerful and exaggerated; in Lebanon it's always dry and dusty and windless and sunny, and when rain comes down – infrequently, in the winter months – it only makes mud and some puddles that dry up by the next morning. But on CKOI, the hosts analyze the storm with the same intensity that Beirut radio used to discuss the political motivations behind militia attacks.

As I pack my purse for the evening, I worry about Omar getting home okay. I decide to call home, to check in. The phone rings, but no one answers, and I get the machine.

"Hi, it's Mama. Where are you? Yallah, I'm coming home now. See you soon."

I hang up. Where could he be? I put on my coat and nod distracted goodbyes at the other sales reps as I walk to the elevators. He was probably in the bathroom or watching TV, I decide. In the evenings, we get calls from salespeople and sometimes we don't answer. He'll get my message.

The sidewalk to the metro is thick with slush that has nowhere to go between snowbanks and buildings. The intersections flood into icy lakes. Cars make waves as they drive past. Traffic lights sway in the wind. My feet are soaked and the metro crowded. This city has been frozen for months, and now it's suddenly humid and releasing all its reihas.

Taking the metro is a peculiar form of suffering. I am quiet and apprehensive as we pause for another delay in the middle of the tunnel. We try to not breathe on each other. Someone coughs. Two stops and fifteen minutes later, I exhale again as I push my way out of the car against crowds of commuters pouring in. I take the escalator up to the ground level where a rush of cold wind instantly turns the sweat on my skin to ice. As I navigate the slippery sidewalk up to our apartment, I curse the city and its sadistic weather.

I must look as beaten down as I feel by the time I get to the apartment because Mr. Saltzman actually looks up from his TV and lowers his glasses. "Okay there?" he calls out.

"It's horrible out," I complain.

"Let's hope we don't lose power," he says, returning to the TV. "Your boy made it in okay, but he doesn't look too hot."

"Okay, thanks," I say, rushing to the elevator.

Ya Allah, I'm tired, hungry, worried, and upset. I find Omar lying in a ball on the couch, lost to a flashing rerun of *Happy Days*, an English show I know he finds boring. Why is he watching it?

"You're home. I was worried. Why didn't you answer the phone?"

On the side table, I see the red light blinking on the answering machine. Omar mumbles something in response, but I can't make it out. I walk over to him and see that his clothes are wet.

"Yaneh, why didn't you change? You're getting the sofa dirty."

He sits up and I see for the first time that he's not just wet but sweating. I feel his forehead, first with my fingers and then with my lips. It's hot to the touch.

"Have you eaten anything?"

Omar shakes his head. I sit down beside him and take him in my arms. "You poor boy," I say, kissing his head. "You're sick and all alone and no one's been here to take care of you. But don't worry, Mama's here now."

He's shivering. His clammy body goes limp in my arms at the sound of my soothing voice. I embrace him more firmly, wanting to squeeze out his fever. It's my fault, I worry. I work too much. I'm never here for him when he needs me. I'm too distracted. But I can't see any other way to take care of us.

I bring over the Panadol and portion out a spoonful. "Yallah, take this. I'll help you get undressed. And then you'll take a quick shower to clean off and warm up. I'll set out your pajamas, and by then you should feel the medicine."

I guide him to his room and he groggily undresses as I get the water just warm enough for his shower. Once I have Omar in the shower, I take a moment to finally put away my purse and jacket and then quickly change. He needs to eat something. *What can we make?* I wonder, looking through the cupboards and fridge. I find a can of Nutri-Fort chicken soup. I pour it into a small pot and bring it to a low boil on the stove. Our small apartment soon smells of chicken and salt. It's a comforting smell. We probably need something more to go with it though. I want him to eat as much as he can to regain his strength. In the freezer, I find one of the Nutri-Fort personal pizzas from work. They aren't very good: their crusts are thin and papery, their toppings bland, and most customers don't reorder them. But Omar thinks they taste like chips when I cook them to a crisp. I tear off the plastic wrap and push one into the oven.

Ya rabi, that's how it goes at times like these. My fears and anxieties shut down just long enough so every decision becomes mechanical. There are times when my body doesn't need all of my mind's capacity to function, when it's better to allow a little bit of myself to fly away, disengage to somewhere else. If ghosts can live without bodies, then why can't our bodies continue on without ghosts?

With dinner on the stove, I can finally take a deep breath for the first time since coming home. I knock on the bathroom door. "Everything okay, Mama?"

"Ai, Mama," he calls back.

"Yallah, there's food waiting when you're done."

I hear the water turn off and go into the kitchen to get the soup in a bowl and the pizza out of the stove for him. Once he finally comes to the table, his skin is pale and glistening once again with fresh sweat.

"Eat. It will make you feel better."

He raises a spoonful to his lips and makes an effort to please me, but his appetite isn't there. I don't really find it edible either; it's bland, ghostly food. Just like that, I've let my son down again. He needs real animal warmth in his stomach, and all I can offer him are convenient boxes brought home from work to avoid grocery shopping in this unlivable weather. I'm losing him, I can see now as he droops in his chair, nibbling at the edges of the stale cardboard pizza. Behind his eyes, all these little disappointments are beginning to add up to a realization. Who bought him those cheap Vêtements 2000 leftovers to get through the winter? They're forming a puddle on the floor by the front door, soaked through. They're the clothes other people throw away precisely because of their uselessness. Who gave him a key and pushed him to rely on himself? He stares blankly at *Wheel of Fortune* on the TV behind me, but inside he must know I'm not up to the task of raising him all by myself.

"Are you feeling too tired, habibi? Do you want to lie down?"

"I don't feel well, Mama. Do I have to go to school tomorrow?"

I look out the window. "Don't worry about tomorrow. Get as much rest as possible and let me worry about everything else."

I set him up on the sofa so he can at least finish his pizza before going off to bed. He's too dazed to do anything other than moan from time to time. I can't afford to miss work tomorrow. I monitor his every move for signs of improvement. Lise Carbonneau has just made an example of two women who've been taking too many sick days. "I have two kids, but you never see me miss a day," she said. That was her challenge to us. Rise to the occasion. Be like me. How can I take a day off and align myself with those other phone operators now that I've been singled out as a sales leader? I bite my nails as I sit there watching him, willing him to miraculously get better by morning.

I wake up to the sound of the wind howling against the windows. Outside, that rain has turned to white dust being whipped in circles over newly cemented sheets of ice. It looks like a different city than the one I finally fell asleep in a few hours ago. Everything has frozen. As I turn on the TV, the morning show is announcing that many schools will be closed. Omar's is among them. "Ya Allah," I utter, staring up at whomever has been kind enough to throw me this minor reprieve.

In my nightgown, I go to Omar's room and sit at the side of his bed. His sheets smell like sweat, but at least he's sleeping soundly. He needs it.

"Habibi," I begin, stroking his hair. He stirs, his eyes cracking open. "How do you feel?"

"I'm so tired, Mama."

"Yallah, go back to sleep. I have to go to work. You stay here no matter what. I'm going to leave some sandwiches for you in the fridge and some medicine to take after lunch. Eat something, watch TV, rest. I'll lock the door behind me and be back for supper. I'll leave my number on the table. Call me for any reason. The secretary will put you through. Okay, ya albeh?"

I give him some Panadol and feel his forehead. It's still warm, but not as bad as last night. He closes his eyes. As I get dressed, I say a little payer. I leave my phone number and other instructions on the kitchen table and put on my coat, toque, mitts, scarf, and boots to go outside. Outside the cold practically shrieks in laughter at my punctured, torn, and salt-stained garments. They've all been abused by the past three months of wear, and they have already resigned to the trash they will soon become. The sidewalks shine in the weak morning streetlights, slippery with the ice that has formed overnight. The world is threatening to twist my ankle at the slightest provocation.

At the office, I'm dismayed to find that half the staff hasn't come to work. Lise Carbonneau, done up to perfection as usual, storms past me as I walk to my desk. "Look how many of them called in sick!" she complains, maybe to me, maybe to someone else, throwing her arms into the air. "The things I do for these people."

I sit at my desk under the fluorescent-white lighting, mostly alone on the sales floor apart from a few other agents who've braved the storm to come in. For the first hour, I prepare progress reports for my client list so that I can better help them understand their journeys. I'll mail them these reports, and once they've arrived, we'll talk through the findings to make sure they're properly understood and I'll communicate the conclusions the clients need to hear: that progress is not always perceptible on the surface, it doesn't always appear where we want to see it, even though it may be happening constantly and incrementally.

I begin making my phone calls at ten, mostly to people who've called the hotline for more information after coming across one of our ads. Today is not a good day for most people to chat; people don't like to talk about weight loss when there's a storm getting in the way of their daily routines. In the afternoon, I switch to calling my regulars. I have Sylvie Leduc on schedule for today. Despite the storm, I have a feeling she'll be open to talking. She usually is.

"Bonjour, Sylvie, c'est Mona. Ça va?" With Sylvie, I know by now to take a friendlier tone. It's not hard. Out of all my clients, she's the one whom I feel genuinely closest to.

"Allô, ma chère Mona. How are you?"

"You've seen this weather outside? It's impossible!"

"It gets worse every year."

"Tell me, how were the last packages?"

"Oh fine. Once I get into the habit, I find it easy. I just look at what I want to eat, add it up for the week, and then divide it by the day. It gives me something to do. I've also started to do an exercise video in the morning."

"You sound like it's going well."

"Two hundred and two as of this morning."

"Sylvie, you're almost at two hundred, that's amazing!"

"I feel different. I look in the mirror, and I even look different."

"I'm so happy for you, Sylvie. You have such courage, and now look what you're doing. Good for you. Tell me, what turned the corner for you?"

"The food helps take care of the distractions of eating. I cook for my family, but I just eat the boxes. Beyond that,

I can say there's two things on my mind that made me realize I needed to change."

"What are they? You need to share your secret for success."

"Oh I wouldn't recommend it to anyone else. It's too painful. I realized that if my husband was cheating on me so much that he felt he could just tell me, then I really was on my own, and something in that opening freed me to only worry for myself. Before his little confession, I have to admit I was caught in an old way of thinking. I was in submission; I let him take the lead on everything: where we lived, what kind of car I drove, whether I should work or not, how to raise the boys. I thought he'd be more sat-isfied that way, you know, with traditional family values, and that he would leave me alone. But all that happened is he got exasperated with all that responsibility and began to resent me. He was desperate to find a way out of the lifestyle he had wanted, the life he made me fit into in the first place, so that he could be happy. And it didn't work. And after that episode we all remember so well, Christmas Day in the kitchen, when he told me what he was doing, all I could remember thinking behind my smile was, *You're such an idiot. I put all my faith in you, and you have no idea what you're doing. I'm married to a loser.* He was pathetic, and he made me pathetic too, and he had turned my body into the body of all his little failures. And so I said to my-self, *I'm not going to do that for him anymore.*"

"How is your marriage now?"

"The bastard is still here. He doesn't know where to go. All that time he'd been thinking about how to tell me, he never thought about what would happen after he did. It was almost as if he expected me to break down in front of him, to kneel at his feet and beg him to return to us, like he was such a prize. And I didn't do that. In that moment, I stayed strong and said nothing. I turned inward and decided I was never going to let him into my decision-making again, that he would never have my confidence from that moment on. And ever since I did that, it's been easier to be disciplined about myself."

"Is he still having the affair?"

"I don't know. Maybe. He goes out sometimes, or he's too ready with his reasons for being late. Anyway, I don't care anymore, and I think that weakens him more than anything. It's like you told me, Mona, I am the center of my family, its foundation. You said it, and after a bit I saw it was true. He was the center before, but only because I wanted him to be the center. Ever since we were married. Do you know I got married at nineteen, Mona? I didn't have a choice. I got pregnant after he forced himself on me in the back of his father's car. We're Catholic, so it was put the child up for adoption or get married. My mother shrugged. She said, get it over with and get married. It will be harder the other way. But all these years now, I wonder: Would it have been harder the other way? I love my boys, but I don't even like my husband if I think about it for too long. I don't know if he's actually enjoying his other women now that he knows I know. He's aware I've shut him out, and without me there to dote on him, he seems lost and unhappy. He's moody. Normally I would try to make him feel better, ask what's wrong. But since I know,

I don't ask. I don't go out of my way for him. It makes all the difference."

"See, this is the Sylvie who's been in you this whole time. We can't see her because she's an old idea, a spark that was left behind as life's many questions began to weigh you down. There was once a time when all you had was potential. That's who you've found under your weight now that it's coming off. I congratulate you, Sylvie. You're an inspiration."

"You're the inspiration, Mona. I don't know how I can ever repay you for your counseling. Your words have helped me see things differently. You are special."

"Oh I don't know that I've done that much. Remember, you're doing all the hard work. I just call and chat. It's still a long road. I'll be here for you."

"You're too modest, chérie. You're an angel."

We hang up ten minutes later, as the call reaches its eighteenth minute (which I note in the client log), and I head to the kitchen to make a tea. As I wait for the kettle to boil, I stare out the window at the never-ending storm and think about what Sylvie said. Yaneh, I married young too. Halim never forced himself on me. How could anyone build a family on that violation? I wonder how my marriage would have turned out without a war to violate it instead. If Halim and I had the chance to be bored, lead ordinary lives. Would we have grown to resent each other?

Ya rabi, these phones and the worlds they let in. Problems show up, but there's always too much going on. How you see the problem depends entirely on the life you've been living and how many other problems you have underway. This is why it's important to let the clients talk, allow them to describe their lives and articulate what makes them ache, in their own words. I feel good about myself for having helped Sylvie even a little, without ever meeting her. Yaneh, I wonder what she looks like.

The electric kettle boils. I steep my tea and throw out the tea bag. As I walk back to my desk, I see that a few more agents have shown up to work, but the office is still much less busy than usual.

A moment after I sit down, the receptionist walks over. "Muna, you've got a personal call on line 2. He says he's your son. You never said you had children!"

I rush along the icy sidewalks, with my gloved hand holding up the hood of my coat against the wind as snow fingers into my clothes any way it can. I wedge my way onto the next busy train, hold on to the railing and stare blankly at the back of another passenger's coat in my face. Yaneh, I stare at nothing, a meaningless pattern, as the train lurches through the tunnel in fits and starts, as I hope against hope that Omar can make it till I get there. There are times when it's easy to believe in yourself, but all that means is that you're overdue for a crisis of faith. The kindness of life never sticks around for long.

As the train stalls again and I yearn to leave my body, I recall a story Halim told me one night when we were in our storage locker, lying on our mattress, huddled in the sheets and whispering so we wouldn't disturb our neighbors and all the children sleeping in their cages. I was bored, and he was carving one of his little wooden animals, and I said, "Yallah, tell me a story."

And he said, "What kind of story?"

And I said, "Any kind of story. Tell me about the most beautiful thing you ever saw."

So he told me a story. "When I was young, I caught po-lio," he began. "My legs weakened and then my entire body. For days, I could barely move. I had a fever. I was so hot, I felt like electricity trapped in a wire. The doctor came, and he told my mother that my chances were fifty-fifty, and that the next two days were critical. I was paralyzed. I lay in bed and floated in and out of consciousness. At times I was lucid, and at others I was lost. I began to drift. I drifted out of my body. I saw myself from outside, as if my face was pressed up against my own cheek. I felt the clamminess of my face, the poison heat of my breathing. I saw that I looked pale. I held on to my own shoulders to stay close. I felt like I was on water, like I was quietly floating away. I remember how I lay on my back and let the calm sea take me, and fog settled around me, replacing the blanket on my bed. *This is it*, I said to myself. *I'm little. I have no way to fight or understand this, and so I will let it take me.* Yaneh, I let myself go and became one with the moment. I floated away, and I was so small that I barely registered a ripple. My life had left no meaning behind. The sea beneath me black-ened and the haze above me whitened. I thought to myself, *I am literally the only thing in existence that can separate these two colors, and once I'm gone, everything will turn to gray.* I remember feeling very worried that this responsibil-ity had come down to me, a sick child. I began to cry; its weight felt so heavy. And then I felt an old hand touch my little fingers. Weakly, I lifted my head and saw my *teta*. She had died before I was born, and even though I'd never seen her before, right away I knew it was her. She was waist-deep in the water next to me. She had the same electricity as me. Through the touch of her hand, she communicated everything I needed to calm down. I knew that I would never be alone. I saw that some people stay with you even after they're gone. They watch over you. As I floated in the water, my grandmother took my hand and led me back to where my body lay in the bed. It wasn't my time, she said. I woke up soon after that, and then I began to get better. I never forgot my grandmother's face. After that day, I no longer felt like the same person. The doctor said the disease changed me, but I knew secretly it was my grandmother and not polio."

The metro doors open, and I push my way out, not caring who I offend anymore. I'm exhausted from trying so hard all the time to accommodate others, only to keep sliding back. This country has an undertow, I think bitterly, an imperceptible death.

I unlock the door to the apartment. My hand shoots up immediately to cover my nostrils against the smell. Omar's been vomiting in a place that hasn't been aired out for months. Taking off my coat, I fear this smell will sit in the curtains for weeks to come.

"Omar habibi," I call out. "I'm home. How are you?"

He moans from the sofa. I walk over and touch his forehead. He's still pale and sweaty.

"Okay, Mama's here and we're going to make this all better." I go to the kitchen and return with a cold glass of water. "Here, have this." I then help him sit up, and after he's had a sip, I help him peel his sticky T-shirt off, dampen a towel in cold water, roll it up, and press it against his shoulders and back to clean him and cool him down. "Yallah, hold this towel to your head if it makes you more comfortable. I'm going to clean the mess."

I hunt for the location of the vomit, which is splattered all over the shower and across the bathroom tiles. I fill a bucket with bleach and water, find the mop. Still in work clothes, I begin to mop up the floor. Ya Allah, thankfully the bathroom is tiny, but it breaks my heart to imagine Omar in here all alone, afraid that he'll throw up. I remember how scary it is to throw up as a child, the restlessness and helplessness of it all. I rinse the shower with bleach and let the hot water run with the fan on to siphon out the smell.

Returning to Omar, I find him lying back down on his side, the wet towel fallen to the floor. As I pass my fingers through his hair, I silently run through what more I can do to help him. I've never seen him this weak. I hope he doesn't have polio like his father. Could a child catch polio in a Canadian school? There's so much I still don't know about this place. I don't want him to die because of my ignorance. A tear rolls down my cheek. I should take him to a doctor, I decide, wiping it away. Looking out the window, I see the city is still screaming at me to stay indoors, away from its gusting winds and icy streets and hours of waiting at its crowded emergency rooms.

If we stay at home, I don't know what else to give him but the little medicine that's left in this over-entrusted bottle of Panadol. I have nothing to offer but the food and rest his body won't accept. *But what if he gets worse?* I wonder. *What if he dies?* I think again. I already took a chance going to work, and it blew up in my face. I can't be trusted to make the right decision.

Not knowing what else to do, I call Mr. Saltzman.

"Saltzman here," he answers after a few rings.

"Hello, it's Muna Heddad in 513."

"Yes?"

"I'm afraid this is quite embarrassing, but I honestly don't know who else to call in this situation. My son is sick with a high fever and vomiting, and I don't know what to do."

"Take him to a doctor."

"I want to. But with the weather, I worry. He's so weak. It might make things worse. What would someone from here do?"

"Okay, okay. Listen, I understand. Sit tight. Let me see about some things and get back to you."

Without knowing what he means, I thank him and hang up. There, I've reached out to this bitter world and asked for help. I soak the washcloth again, sit on the couch, and press it to Omar's temple as he writhes against the cushions. I can't stop thinking of Halim's story. I want him to live. Without Omar, I could not go on. I would be done.

Ten minutes later, there's a knock at the door. I get up to answer it, expecting Mr. Saltzman. Instead, there's a Black man standing there, a brown leather bag in hand.

"Are you the mother with the sick child?" he asks me. I nod.

"I am Amadou. Saltzman sent me. I live in the building."

"Why would he send you?"

"I'm a medical student at the university. He knows I'm training to be a pediatrician. Can I see your son?"

I let him in. "My apologies for the smell."

Amadou steps inside. "Hello there, young man. What seems to be the problem?"

Omar moans.

"Can you help him sit up?" he asks me.

Amadou bends down to take a closer look at Omar. He opens his bag and pulls out some instruments. He checks his pupils with a penlight, checks his mouth and tonsils with a tongue depressor, and then listens to his chest and back with a stethoscope. He takes Omar's temperature.

"He's had a high temperature for how long?"

"About twenty-four hours now."

"And he has no appetite, vomits, is weak like this?"

"Yes."

Amadou stands up. "Then my guess is your son has a stomach flu, which is unfortunately common at this time of year."

"What is that? Is it dangerous?"

"It's a seasonal virus." He looks around for the first time and then asks, "How long have you been in Canada?"

"Since last summer."

"Okay then, you and your son don't have the immune system to handle these kinds of viruses just yet. You're prime candidates. My first year here from Senegal, I caught it bad too."

"What should I do?"

"There's nothing to do, really, unless he begins to dehydrate. Give him that Panadol, or Tylenol or aspirin, for the fever. Otherwise, as long as his fever doesn't go too high, he needs to rest and drink liquids until it passes. Three to five days, maybe longer."

"Can he eat?"

"If he has an appetite, then yes."

"What can I feed him to make it better? What should I avoid?"

"What does he eat now? Anything out of the ordinary?"

"I give him food from my work."

"Where do you work?"

"At a weight-loss center. They have their own line of food for diet plans. It's healthy for you. It's been modified to give you more of its nutrients and less of its fat." I show him some of the boxes.

"I would stop giving him this," Amadou says, handing it back. "It's junk with a different taste and texture. It gives the body nothing to work with, as well as a few things it doesn't need at all. It's not suitable for a growing boy. In fact, I would recommend you stay away from it too."

"But it helps so many people lose weight. I've read the studies."

"Well, this is debatable," Amadou says. "Nothing but bread and water for twenty-four hours, and then go back to introducing only real food, little by little. Avoid spices. Call me if the vomiting or stomach pains persist past tomorrow."

"Okay. Thank you, Doctor," I say, walking him to the door.

"I'm not a doctor yet," he reminds me. "At least not here."

"You are a doctor to me."

"Inshallah," he smiles.

"That's right, inshallah," I smile back.

"I'm in 802 if you need me." He dictates his phone number, and I write it down.

"Thank you, Amadou," I say again as we stand at the door. "Vraiment, merci."

"Plenty of rest, plenty of water," he reminds me as he walks down the hall to the elevator.

I go back inside and can't help but think the world isn't as bad as I made it out to be earlier. I asked for help, and I was given help. I am grateful to everyone and to no one, to Mr. Saltzman and to Amadou and to the spirit of humanity. I sit back down next to Omar and take a deep breath, relieved.

"Tayeb, you're going to be okay, ya habibi," I say, patting Omar's leg. "It's just a seasonal virus. Yallah, let's get you into bed. You need rest and water."

I help him into bed and think I'm not such a bad mother after all. A doctor's advice has calmed me down. Even Omar seems to doze more easily now that he's been examined. I let my emotions get the best of me, I think to myself after he's settled. Quietly, I undress in front of the TV, and, with my nose plugged, I step into the shower I just washed. I stand under the steam of hot water and wait for my pores to release all the day's indignities. I stay there for a long time, really just relieved and grateful to be warm. When I step out, I call out to the mirror, "Where are you when I need you?" But this time I get no reply.

I'm in no mood to push myself any further today. I realize I'm hungry. In my pajamas, I fix myself a quick sandwich and a cup of tea. I can't bring myself to open any Nutri-Fort boxes after what Amadou told me. Yaneh,

I don't know if he's right, but I've always been suspicious of how that food tastes. After I'm done, I place my plate in the sink, open up my sofa bed and turn on the TV. Even though it's only eight, I am ready for this day to end. I check in on Omar one more time. He's asleep. He must never be fully comfortable all that time he's home alone. I like to think he's fine, but it only makes it easier for me to leave him here for long stretches.

I find a sitcom on one of the French channels, turn it down to low, and let its imagery lull my eyes. One show ends and another begins. This one I recognize immediately: it's a rerun of a comedy show called *Les Brillant* that airs every weeknight. If not for the color of my skin, I think I look like Françoise Lemieux, with her thin nose and straight hair. They're like the office ladies. They chat and joke about things only people from here can understand and appreciate. Nothing much happens on the show except for a lot of talking in a restaurant, a library, a school, a kitchen. The humor is fast and subtle. I don't pay attention to any of it. I fall asleep this way, letting the TV fill in the silence and keep my mind distracted. I dive backwards into a silly dream where I'm on *Les Brillant*. All of a sudden I'm chatty and funny, and the other characters treat me like I'm the best part of the show.

I don't wake up again until four in the morning, when I hear Omar stirring in the next room. The TV is washed out in snow. I ignore it and listen. Is he awake? I hear a moaning. Quietly, I get out of bed and walk over to the door of his room. He's talking in his sleep. I slip over to the side of his bed and look down. His face is cast in the glow of the city lights outside. I sit down at his side and watch his lips move. They don't make a sound, but every once in a while he groans or swoons. I touch his head: he's dry and burning. I don't want to wake him, even as I get up to soak his washcloth in cold water. I lay it gently across his forehead. His fingers light upon my hand. The water drips down the side of his face. I see a puddle form in the socket of his eye. And then he startles awake and sits up in a start, clenching my hand.

"It's okay, ya habibi. I'm right here. You were having a dream, that's all."

He looks around the room and slumps over in disappointment.

"What's wrong?" I ask.

"In my dream, I saw Baba," he says. "He came to see me, and he held my hand."

"That's love," I say. I kiss his head. "You never forget some people, and they never forget you."

I'm worried. I see that Omar is growing irritated with me and how I'm always at work. Over the past two days, he's spent all his time alone in the apartment. When his fever started to come down, he regained some of his energy, and it's made him bored and resentful. For the first time since we arrived in this country, he's moody. He has outbursts. Ever since he woke up from that dream where he held his father's hand, he's realized he's dissatisfied with the way things are.

Ya Allah, what can I do? Once I finally lie down for a few hours' sleep, I stare at the ceiling and think about how I can make it up to him after my French class the next day. I've already left Omar alone in the apartment for three whole days, and tomorrow I will do it all over again for my first Saturday French class in the church basement. Tonight, after working at the office all day and then over-caring for Omar to quench my guilt, I've stayed up till three in the morning to prepare my first lesson at the new location. Winnie says I can expect twenty-four students. To the hum of the TV, I sit at the kitchen table, my eyes red and raw from lack of sleep, devising a lesson plan to suit more students and our new room, where I'll have a portable chalkboard and enough chairs for everyone.

I yawn. I put away my work, lie down on the sofa bed, and curl up into a ball. The voices from the TV blend in with the voices in my head. Numbed by the effort of it all, I hear voices all around me.

"Why'd you visit him?" I ask, sleepily. "You're confusing him."

"He was in need." I feel an arm around me, the warmth of another body.

"Was he in danger of dying?"

"No. But he's wandering away further than he's ever gone. He's getting lost."

"All this was going on as I slept in the other room. I've never felt so far away from him. I'm losing him."

"I never felt closer to him," says Halim, "so able to help."

"And now you've held Omar's hand." My eyelids feel so heavy. "All this work I've put in to help him forget you, erased."

"I will always be there, in his origins. It was never going to be any other way."

"But now he's bitter," I say, losing consciousness as I let out my last words.

When I wake up, it's already light out, and Omar is sitting at the kitchen table in his pajamas, eating a bowl of cereal. He has the wooden horse standing right next to the bowl, as if to say, "Look, I'm having breakfast with Baba instead." I sit up, my eyes swollen, my hair matted against the side of my face.

"You're eating," I say, my voice croaking. "That's good. You must feel better."

He nods as milk slips off his spoon and onto the table.

"Be careful around Mama's papers."

Without saying anything, he slides the bowl over to one side of the table and moves to the far chair, taking the horse with him. He's staring at the TV, but it's not even on. He's upset. I get up and gather my things so they're not in his way.

"Eat your breakfast in my bed, if you like," I offer. I turn on the TV for him. "I have to get ready anyway. After I come back, I'm all yours."

He shrugs, picking up his bowl, and moves over to the bed. "I'll be fine," he says.

"Oh, good." I try to smile.

Yaneh, children have a strange way of interpreting things. I don't have time to address it now. I have to get ready.

The class is a success. I could not let myself fail when Winnie has taken this big risk bringing me into her church community. I push through our two-hour session on what little adrenaline I have left and the bundled nerves that have built up in all my limbs. The class is no longer only women who need language skills for work. At twenty-four students, I have several men in the group too, as well as some teenagers and even a senior citizen. When I leave the church basement, I have four hundred and eighty dollars in wrinkled bills. I'm having a hard time believing I made this much for a couple hours' work. That Nutri-Fort commission has continued to inch up every week, and with these French classes approaching their third month, I've managed to save a lot of money since the New Year. I can't help but be proud of myself, even if no one, not even Omar, recognizes what I've done. I have to share this moment with him, to make him understand why we sacrifice like we do.

When I get back to the apartment, I move aside the carved horse and dirty dishes and lay out all the money on the table for Omar to see.

"See what I do for you?" I announce. "I'm trying to make our lives better."

Money gets his attention. He looks down at it, impressed. "That's a lot," he says.

"There's more." I pull down the shoebox and say, "Yallah, let's help Mama count this."

He puts together piles as I've instructed, adding them up to a hundred each while taking time to look at each bill carefully for its number, color, and drawings. It takes him some time, and by the end we see there's almost fifteen hundred dollars in my shoebox above the fridge. *Mabrouk, Muna*, I think to myself, looking down at the piles. Now that I see it in front of me, I can't believe I was able to live on so little for so long. And I have to admit that even though this city has fought off my every advance, there are nevertheless people here whose random kindness has made all the difference.

"Can we buy something?" Omar asks.

"What do you want to buy?"

"Let's go for pizza at the restaurant downstairs."

I touch his head. "Are you feeling better?"

"Ai."

He's wanted to go to that student pizzeria ever since we moved into this building. I don't think it looks very tasty – the pizza here has too much cheese and too much dough – but I can't say no to this boy after what I've put him through, so I say, "Okay, that's what we'll do. Go take a shower, comb your hair, and find some nice clothes."

"What should I wear?"

"I'll lay out some clothes for you," I say. We're back to normal, I think. Inshallah.

A while later, I take Omar down to the pizza restaurant, and we sit in a booth, out of place among all the students there, joking and chatting over their shared dinners. I let him do the ordering. He carefully selects a medium pepperoni pizza. "With no vegetables," he specifies. "And a Coke."

"No vegetables. Gotcha." The waitress winks at him. "Anything to drink for you, ma'am?"

"Water, thank you."

The waitress walks over to the kitchen window and calls in the order. We sit there quietly for a few minutes and listen to the sounds of the restaurant: the chef's bell for orders to be picked up, the cash register's sliding drawer, radio hits in the background.

"How's school?" I ask.

Omar shrugs. "Okay, I guess."

"There's only a few months left. I'll probably have to talk to your teacher again soon. Are you doing better on your work?"

"I have some papers for you to sign in my Duo-Tang. I forgot to tell you."

"How long have they been sitting there?" I say, suddenly concerned. "You should always tell me these things when they come up."

"You're never home," he says. He looks out the window as his Coke arrives.

I reach over the table and take his hand in mine, the way I always do to get his full attention. "Ya habibi, I'm here now."

I can feel his hand wanting to pull away.

"You need to know this isn't forever. We're just in this situation temporarily. We're going to move soon."

"Again?"

"What do you mean? Of course again! Did you think that tiny apartment is going to be home? We just landed there. We need to move on, build our proper home. You can have your own bedroom."

"I have my own bedroom."

"Well, I don't. I want one too. I know it hasn't been easy. Sometimes, there's only so much I can do. But I'm trying. Anyway, it will be exciting to go look at new apartments. Think of the possibilities."

The pizza arrives, and for a few minutes that takes up all his attention. The way he eats, I get the impression he doesn't want to talk about any of this.

"Well, things will get better from now on," I continue, just so we don't sit in silence. "I wanted us to have this pizza because I would like to thank you for being so understanding. You've been so brave. Coming here to Canada, just the two of us, to make this new life hasn't been easy."

"What if I hate it here?" he asks quietly.

"You're so young. You have a lifetime of possibilities here. Your feelings will change."

"You keep telling me what to think, Mama."

"I'm being strong for you. You're not an adult. How can you understand anything we're going through?" The sudden vehemence in my voice catches Omar off guard and his lower lip begins to quiver. My hand shoots out to his.

"I'm sorry, ya habibi. I love you so much, and I'm working hard so we can dig ourselves out from how bad the past six months have been. I know it's not easy, that it's been one of the most difficult years of our lives and it doesn't seem like we've gained anything by coming here. But it's just this one year, and in time inshallah, you'll see this year for how it fits in, our chance to start again."

"I don't want to start again. I want our old life with Baba and the rest of the family."

"What do you remember of your father?" I can hear my voice snap again.

His shoulders spring back. He hesitates. "I remember a lot. I think about him all the time."

"Then why do you never say anything? Why do you always act like you don't remember him? Why must I always guess what you think about your father and what happens at school? It's too hard to get this information out of you. I already have to work so hard at everything else. Why make me work at giving you the love you want?"

"I don't want love."

A tear wells up in the corner of my eye as I gaze at him. "I miss him too." I finally say. "My life hasn't been great either. What do you want, ya albeh? Tell me."

"I don't know," he says.

"We've been given a gift. Our old lives are useless to us now; you may think we left them behind, but the truth is they abandoned us. If you're old enough to say such things, then you might as well know: you and me, we're not wanted by anyone other than us. There is no old life calling us back. It spit us out. One day the worst of it will fade, become details in our background, and then maybe you'll have a good story to tell about what makes us different than everyone else."

Much to Omar's relief, the waitress walks over. "Can I get you two anything else? Coffee? Dessert?"

"Thank you, no," I say. "Just the bill and the rest of this to go."

I turn back to Omar sitting across from me, and I see he's crouched back in the booth, as far away from me as he can get. I take a deep breath and realize I've said a lot, too much. I wasn't aware that I was so upset, but now that I've started talking out loud about all these things for the first time, I see that I've been holding back so much I need to let out of me and that maybe I have to work so hard for my son's love because he sees me as someone who isn't really there.

"I'm sorry, ya habibi. This is all so hard on you, and on me. You're all I have. I live for you."

He looks at me as if he wants to disappear from the embarrassment of having me utter those words at him in public. He's getting too old to tell me he loves me. I hope to God he still does love me, that I'm not too late. I've been working too hard, and I missed the moment a wall went up between us.

The waitress comes back, and I quickly leave exact change and tip so we can go. As we walk back through the lobby to our apartment, I feel sorry for myself and because of the choices I've made for us. I can help strangers who call a hotline number, but I can't help my only family.

"I'm not going to miss living here once we go," I say, changing the subject.

"Can we live somewhere with a backyard?" he says, relieved to follow this simpler line of dreaming.

"Tayeb, I don't see why not. We can go look and see what there is."

"Next weekend?"

"Yaneh, soon." I ruffle his hair and pull him in for a kiss. His body softens, and he allows me to draw him close. I am grateful for the permission. "You'll see. I'm sorry for putting you through this past year. You did great. Things will be so much better once we move."

I hope I'm not making an empty promise.

Omar has gone back to school, the transition to the church basement is behind me, and I've done a big grocery shop and finally filled the fridge with fresh food so we don't eat boxes all the time. Yaneh I can say I've taken care of a few crises these past weeks! Now, I must let Mona get back on the phone and make her calls without distraction. It's time to check in with Louis Laflamme. I've been worried for him since last time, when he sounded erratic and lost. I pitied him for reaching out to me the way he did. Poor man. Before I get on the line, I resolve to be more distant, to not give him any room for misinterpretation, but without making him feel any worse.

The phone rings three times before he picks up.

"Hydro Québec, department des comptes. Monsieur Laflamme à l'appareil."

"Oui bonjour, Monsieur Laflamme. This is Mona calling from Nutri-Fort."

"Oh hello, Mona. Wonderful to hear from you. How are you?"

"Me? I'm fine. I think we may have had our last big storm, so I'm feeling optimistic about change. How about you, Louis? You sound like you're doing well."

"You know what, Mona. I guess I am."

"Wonderful. Did you get the last order?"

"I did. I'm enjoying all the selections."

"Are you finding it easier to stay on the program?"

"I am."

"That's great, Louis. You were struggling last time. I'm happy to hear you've turned a corner. I can even hear it in your voice."

"To be honest, I do feel like I've turned a corner. You gave me some good advice last time."

"Well, thank you for saying that, Louis. I'm happy to hear you found something useful in our discussion."

"Remember when you told me to stop eating at the casse-croûte, to have my boxes at home and just go there for coffee after? You know, for the chats. Well, I thought to myself, come on, Louis, what do you have to lose? I mean, let's be honest: I was feeling so bad about myself, I figured something has to happen. Between you and me, Mona, last time we spoke I thought there was a pretty good chance I wasn't going to make it to our next call. So instead of sitting in my apartment with these ideas running circles in my head, one night I give it a try. I eat a few boxes and then go to the casse-croûte and sit down at the counter, right across from Josée. That's the waitress. She's not too much younger than me, maybe five years at most. She says to me, 'The usual?' And I say, 'Um, no.' She places her hands at her hips and stares at me. She's a big girl like me, sturdy, takes no shit. She's trying to figure me out. So she says, 'What'll it be then?' And I say, 'Just a coffee.' And she says, 'Nobody comes to a casse-croûte for the coffee, mon cher.' And for the first time I actually hear myself say it out loud."

"What did you say?" I ask, captivated.

"I say, 'I'm on a diet. My doctor says I can't keep gaining weight, and I have to try something different. So I'd just like to order a coffee.'"

"What happened next?"

"What happens next is really the kicker. She puts her hand on mine, pats it, and says, 'Good on you.' And then she gets me a coffee. She starts telling me things that I've never heard her say before. She tells me how she's been working there for almost two decades, ever since she was twenty-seven, and that she's seen a lot of regulars sit right where I'm sitting over the years, and each one of them has withered away into a shell of his former self. She said her father was one of them. She actually says, 'I'm proud of you.' Every time I've come in after that, she brings me the one black coffee right away, no questions asked. And she talks to me whenever she's not taking orders. Soon it's like she expects me to show up. She wants to know how it's going. I told her about the boxes and the system. She even says that it looks like it's working."

"Oh Louis, that's great news. What number are you seeing on the scale these days?"

"I'm down fourteen actually."

"Wonderful work. I'm so happy for you. It helps when we know someone else is paying attention, doesn't it?"

"To be honest, the other evening when I was getting ready to go home, she says, 'I'll make you a home-cooked meal that's better for you than any of those boxes.' She's invited me over for dinner."

"Oooh, sounds romantic," I say, feeling I can get away with being a little playful now that his attention is on another woman.

"It does, doesn't it? It's tomorrow night. What can I do to prepare?"

"Just be yourself, Louis. Remember, your honesty and humility are what she found interesting in the first place."

I hang up the phone soon after, happy for Louis. For the rest of the day at the office, I'm in a better mood than I've been in for a long time. I really can get dramatic, I think to myself as I go over what had truly bothered me about the last few weeks. In the place of all those obstacles, I now see challenges I've overcome.

Tayeb, maybe it's the end of winter that has this effect on a person. The girls around the office are saying we may have made it through the last of the big storms. We're almost at the end of March, and spring should show up any day now.

"You'll see, Muna," says Esther, our bookkeeper who moved here from Haiti a few years before I did. We're both making our afternoon coffees in the office kitchen. "The temperature will go up one day soon, and the air, it will change. After the winter we've just had, it'll become your favorite time of year."

She never talked to me before, but these last few weeks she's been saying hello and acting friendlier. At the beginning of the month, Lise posted an announcement to the office bulletin board, so now everyone knows that I was the office's top salesperson for February. Who knew it would get so much attention! The Nutri-Fort vice president in Toronto sent me a personally signed card with my bonus check. Practically all the ladies have come by my desk to congratulate me. People now say hello to me and use my name. We chat in the elevators.

"I've found it hard, it's true," I admit to Esther. "Before moving here, I never imagined weather could be like this."

"You learn to live with it," says Stéfanie, an older lady who joined the sales team a month ago and who drinks green tea instead. "You adapt, you stop noticing it after a while. I never let it get to me. But I'm from here, unlike you two ladies, so I have nothing to compare it to."

Something is changing, I realize. I'm having a casual conversation in the office kitchen. I'm okay with Stéfanie acknowledging that I'm not from here; at least it's out in the open, not something I have to hide or compete against. Now that I've been working here four months, I feel comfortable around these women. If I relax, I can allow myself to be natural and unguarded with them now. I've seen them break down over clients, rush home for emergencies, work through illnesses. And they've seen me through the same. I feel myself equal to these women now, and inshallah they treat me as an equal in return.

"Well, time to get to my calls," I say, collecting my mug.

"You go rake in that cash, sweetie," Esther says, not looking up from her magazine.

I smile and touch her shoulder on the way out. I like Esther. She has six children, the oldest one is nineteen and the youngest four, and she's still here every morning, flipping through the staff magazines and making small talk even as she updates and tabulates all the client accounts. I like Stéfanie too. She's my mother's age, has gray dreadlocks, and works here because she got divorced and now has to make her own living for the first time just when many of her friends from her previous life are planning to retire. She told me all this the very first time we crossed paths in this kitchen. Tayeb, she's just an open book like that. Lise says clients like the intonation of wisdom in her old voice. She calls Stéfanie *ma tante funky* and does a little dance with her arms every time she says it. Stéfanie seems to relish the name and has begun referring to herself as everyone's funky aunt.

I go back to my desk and organize my files for the morning as my coffee cools. Omar is finally back at school, and on the corner of my desk are the French and English newspapers, which I've started buying again now that we're looking for an apartment. Yaneh, it's given us something to look forward to and to work on together. When we first moved into our building last August, I was in such a rush that we didn't know where we'd landed or what it meant. The landlords of this city threw up walls in front of my every expression of interest, and I had no sense of what it all meant. I was turned away because I have a child, I have no husband, I am an Arab, I have no job, I have no history – their lists are endless. In the end, I could only find expensive apartments in the McGill Ghetto, where the international students all lived, though I didn't know that's what it was at the time. After seven months, we at least have a better sense of how this place works, and that makes all the difference.

WHAT WE BURY LIVES ON AND ON

~

Those snowbanks that long ago turned to brown ice like my heart are finally melting again. These sidewalks are no longer treacherous. We can unwrap the tight scarves around our faces. It's finally spring in Montreal. Downtown office workers are coming up from the underground city, taking off their toques and unzipping their coats. I'd forgotten that feeling of fresh air. The cold has been stinging my cheeks for so long I no longer find it feels so bad.

Today when I open a window in our apartment for the first time this year to let out the dead air of our central heating and collective cooking, I realize how tired I am from this journey I've endured. Ya Allah, I'm worn down from living among the discarded leftovers of other people's lives. I can no longer ignore that I sleep in the drooping cheek of a sofa bed that's been slept in by how many strangers before me. Life is telling me that there's someone in line behind me, somewhere out there, worse off than me, who needs it more.

It's the first week of April, and the time has finally come to start calling all those numbers in the newspapers and find us a home. I go downstairs and knock on Mr. Saltzman's door.

"Come on in, Muna," he says, waving me in without looking away from the episode of *All in the Family* on his TV set. "How can I help you?"

After placing my weekly rent in cash on his desk, I say what I have to say. "Mr. Saltzman, I'd like to officially give you three months' notice that I'll be moving out."

He looks up at me. "Sure thing. But you don't have to give me three months. You rent by the week."

"I just want to make sure I have enough time to find the right place for us."

"You know, I may have a two-bedroom opening up soon if you're interested. I always like to hold on to a good tenant."

"Thank you. You've been so helpful already. But it's time to move on to a place where we can settle in."

"Yeah, I get it," he says, standing up. "Go live in a family neighborhood where your kid can have a park and a good school. You don't need to live in a building with all these international students."

"Well, I'd like to stay close enough to the metro so I can get to work."

"In three months, I'm sure you'll find something. But not everyone will be as nice as me. The landlords in this city are sharks."

"I know," I say, smiling. I've left seven messages already, of which only two were returned. After some initial questions revealed that I have a child, both told me their apartments were already rented. "I've learned that much in the time I've been looking."

"Sure, you pay attention," he says. "Anyways, good luck with it. I'm sure you'll be fine."

Tayeb, there are apartments for rent everywhere. I know Montreal's streets and neighborhoods, its divisions between east and west, where to speak French and where to work with my broken English, what types of properties are owned by les pure laines and which ones are owned by les Anglos, where the students rent, where the immigrants live. At the beginning, I thought it would be okay to land next to a university because they have everything a person needs within walking distance, and there are usually a lot of apartments available. Others from Lebanon, I now see, don't even bother to live downtown. They live north of the city, near the very last stops of the green line or across the North Shore in Laval, far away from everyone and everything. On my own, I can't afford to be that far away.

As well as scouring the For Rent pages in all the newspapers, now that the weather allows it, I spend the weekend walking through different neighborhoods like the Plateau and Shaughnessy Village, which are also in walking distance of downtown, in search of the red-and-white or orange-and-black À LOUER signs posted on front balconies. Newspapers only offer a small portion of what's actually available. The real treasures are these balcony postings that are only ever up for a few days to a few weeks. I've put Omar in charge of looking out for these signs as we walk along. Whenever he spots one, we write down all the information.

We walk to the nearest dépanneur or casse-croute, where there's usually a pay phone outside or in the back. Omar and I squeeze into the booth, he reads the number out loud as I dial, and then he drops in the quarter so the call will go through. On the rare chance I catch someone on the other end and confirm the listing, I tell them that I'm just down the street. I've found it's easier to get to see an apartment if a landlord knows I'm already in the neighborhood. Once I'm at their door, they can't turn me away as easily inshallah. They have to confront the fact that I'm a human being with feelings and I can't be made to go away with just any excuse.

That's when we get to walk through the narrow hallway of someone else's home. Most Montreal apartments are long and gloomy, their kitchens at the back, their rooms built side by side, connected by corridors too narrow for bringing in anything but cheaply made furniture that has to be assembled once it's there. If I think the insides are too run-down – if there's mold or water damage in the bathroom, if the cabinet doors are hanging off their hinges in the kitchen, if there are abandoned trash bags that look like they've been on the back balcony since last autumn – then I don't say much. Yaneh, I just nod, say thank you, and leave. But if the apartment looks promising, then I begin to talk about myself. I mention my work. That's when I find out what's really going to happen. They say, "The apartment was just seen by someone else who wants to take it. Would you be willing to pay more?" Or, "The building's actual owner wants anyone interested to fill out an application form." Sometimes I get, "The floors are thin and the neighbors downstairs can't listen to a child running around all day and night." Any excuse will do. They know I can't and won't question it. C'est une langue secrète, the art of understanding what isn't said.

We always come home at the end of the weekend defeated by what we've been told. We always hold out hope for the remaining numbers we've called; every call left out there is potentially another rope dangling down to pull us up into our next lives.

It's not until our fifth weekend of walking around the streets that we finally stumble across something promising. It comes in the form of an À LOUER sign not three blocks from where we live. We find it on one of the tree-lined residential streets in the northern end of the McGill Ghetto as we're walking back from a series of disappointing viewings some twenty minutes away in the boulevard Saint-Laurent area. We've walked this way before, but a sign's never been posted, and so I've never paid attention to the building.

"Should we call it?" Omar asks as we stand out front.

I look around. It's really a beautiful street, wide, well maintained, one-way so it doesn't get much traffic. The triplex itself is freshly painted, with big bay windows. "Tayeb, I think this is too expensive for us."

"Oh probably not," says a voice from inside, and it's then I notice the window on the second floor is wide open and inside behind the screen there's an old man, maybe in his seventies, about Mr. Saltzman's age, who looks like he's remodeling.

"Excuse-moi, monsieur," I call up. "How much is the rent?"

"Four fifty a month," he calls down in English. "Four and a half. Wanna take a look?"

I'm surprised by the offer because the viewing we've just come from didn't even want to let us in after opening the door to the horror of a dark-skinned woman and a thin, shaggy-haired boy.

"Yes, it would be very kind of you to let us have a look," I say.

"Come on up then."

The landlord is a short and wiry man, his obviously white hair dyed black and combed back. He meets us on the ground-floor landing and invites us in through one of two old wooden doors. Inside, we find a spacious wood-paneled corridor.

"It's beautiful in here," I say.

"Yeah, it's been in my family for three generations. I do my best to keep it up. The apartment's up on the second floor."

He points to the wooden staircase. In the apartment, all the original moldings and wood trims have been preserved. The hardwood floors, though they've been maintained, have dipped with age in some spots.

"I've just painted," the old man says. It almost sounds like he's trying to sell me on the place.

"It's beautiful," I say, admiring the kitchen tiles and built-in bookshelves in the living room. "When was this built?"

"1887."

"One hundred years old."

"Just about. I've owned it for the last forty. I've renovated the kitchen and bathroom and done some repairs here and there, but I like the old look, so I keep it."

"I've never seen anything like it."

The apartment has large windows all along the back,

with a pair of French doors that open onto a small balcony and stairs leading down to a overgrown back garden bordered by a rotting fence.

"Does the apartment have access to the yard?"

"It's for all three apartments, but no one really uses it. If you want it for your boy, I can mow the lawn."

"And it's available?" I ask, to get it over with. It's at this question that landlords begin to make up excuses about other viewings or having a check in hand from other prospective renters.

"If you have first and last. I usually only get students coming to look, and they can make so much noise, and don't get me started on the damage they leave behind. You look like you'll be quiet and you won't break stuff. Are you an international student?"

"No, I work full-time," I say. "I can pay you the first and last in cash."

"If you're not a student, then I'll also need a reference from your employer."

"I can do that," I confirm, wondering if he's starting to pile on the barriers.

"Okay then. Take a moment to look around. I'll be outside."

I walk slowly around the apartment, trying to imagine if I can see a future here. With its darkened wood panels, its dusty brass chandelier above where a dining table would go, and its large cast-iron heaters under its large windows, the place is older than all the other places I've seen, but those features also give it a charm that reminds me of the black-and-white movies I sometimes watch late at night when I can't sleep. The powder-blue Formica all over the kitchen most likely dates from the fifties or sixties. The appliances are a few decades old as well.

I try to imagine myself here, cooking in this kitchen. There's enough counter space to prepare a proper meal. Across the hall, I can look into what would be Omar's bedroom. I walk into it. It's a good size. The master bedroom is off the living room. It comes with a giant tree as its view. I listen to the apartment: no neighbor's television next door, no stomping feet upstairs, no traffic.

"What do you think?" I ask Omar.

"I like it," he says. "But we don't have any furniture."

"We'll get some. Not all of it right away. But we'll get beds to start, and then work our way to the rest." I take his hand in mine. "Would you be happy here?"

He shrugs. "Sure, I guess."

What I really mean to ask is *Would I be happy here?* Ya rabi, faced with a real prospect, all of a sudden it seems like a risk to move. What if I just end up losing the little I was meant to hold on to? Standing here in this empty living room, that risk is also a thrill. In my head, I'm already locating the closest bus stop, the way to the metro, the walk to the grocery store, Omar's route to school. Staying at the same school will provide him some stability after all these years of changes. I imagine myself hunting for furniture on weekends to fill out all this space. Maybe Mr. Saltzman would sell me some lamps and end tables. The rest I would want to buy new, so it would be all mine. I could be happy here, I decide. This apartment has room enough to let us grow into other people.

"If it's still available," I tell the landlord outside, "I'll take it." I'm half-expecting him to have changed his mind.

"Okay then," he says, taking down the sign that's tied to the porch railing. "I'll get the papers ready. Come back tomorrow and we'll get everything in order. You can give me your reference's number then too. My name's Mike, by the way."

That night after Omar has gone to sleep, as I watch the late-night movie from under my covers, I take hold of Halim's hand and confess, "I want you to know you've kept me strong. This whole time, I've looked to you for willpower and guidance, and you've been there."

"I have nowhere else to go," he says. I hear his little laugh, the air beneath the blanket misting between us.

"You'll always have a home with me, no matter where I go, my love."

He brings my hand to his lips and kisses it. "You don't need anyone to help you."

"That doesn't mean I don't want it."

I close my eyes, and we kiss for a while, absently, more a haunting of closeness than closeness itself. I can make his presence stronger so that he doesn't fade back into the fabric. I can feel his lips in all their softness and the bristle of his unshaven chin. I feel them on my mouth and my cheeks and my nose and my eyes. I let his hand nestle behind my back and pull me closer. On TV, the dramatic swells of the old movie's orchestra bring a pivotal moment to life, and for a moment my whole world drifts into Technicolor. I'm suspended in disbelief. This must be what happiness feels like.

When I wake up alone to a silent screen in the middle of the night, I find my pillow damp, bunched up between my legs. The television's test card screen awaits the beginning of another broadcast day. In the dark, I strip the pillow of its casing and hang it to dry by the open window.

Going into work that Monday I'm a little concerned that I've promised Mike something I might not be able to deliver. I confidently offered him a work reference, without even asking Lise Carbonneau if she's willing to provide me one. I always felt she would, but now that I'm testing this hypothesis, all I can see in my mind is a look on her face that says *I'm shocked you'd even think to take advantage of me that way, you sharmouta.* She enunciates every syllable to make sure I understand the permanent veil of foreignness I'm wearing, which leads to this particularly unfortunate subclass of misunderstanding. I feel like I'm wearing that veil as I arrive at work this morning, as I walk to my desk and set down my bag.

"Bon matin, Muna," chimes Stéfanie from the next desk over. She's already busy typing her notes into a report.

"Yallah hi, ya Stéfanie," I reply, distracted and slipping into the Arabic mindset I diligently suppress at work.

Stéfanie raises her eyebrows, noticing a difference. "It sounds so beautiful how you say it in your language. I feel like I'm on safari," she says, a gleam in her eye that says she's imagining herself on a camel's back in Egypt.

"It brings me pleasure to offer you this small vacation at work."

We both laugh a little and leave it at that.

As I organize my papers for the morning, I keep looking across the room to Lise's door. Ladies file past with folders in their arms. One of the few men who quietly work here pushes a cart of boxed foods from the storage room to the distribution center. Through them all, I spy her closed door. The blinds of her glass wall are drawn. She's either busy or not here yet, and since Lise is always here, she's busy. I put in my first call of the morning and wrap up in fifteen minutes exactly with an order in hand for a two-week meal plan. I'm typing up my order when I see Lise's door open. A middle-aged man and woman, both in gray business suits and carrying briefcases, drift out with her. She's speaking to them in English, which I've never heard her do before, laughing at everything they say as she walks them to the elevators. When Lise returns, she's back to normal, walking intently with unusual poise and the joyless expression her face prefers when she thinks no one else is paying attention. She enters her office, leaving her door open.

What do you think, ya Muna? Is this a good moment? I ask myself, biting my lip. I don't want to catch her in a bad mood. The sooner the better, I decide, getting up.

Even though the door is open, I give her the courtesy of two quick knocks.

"Muna." Lise looks up and smiles. "Come in. Have a seat. Ça va bien, ma poulette?"

"I'm well, thank you, Ms. Carbonneau."

"I'm just going through the April numbers, and I have to say I'm very impressed with the work you're doing here."

I thank her again. "It's really because of the New Year's Resolution campaign. Like you said before, if you make the right moves in January, you can set up the rest of your year to be profitable. I was skeptical at first, but it works."

"You're fantastic. I love your energy."

"Oh, thank you," I say again, blushing. Yaneh, if I thank her one more time, I'll sound like a groveling donkey. I take the opportunity to pivot into my reason for being in her office. "I wanted to ask you, if I may. I want to move apartments soon, and I would like to stay in my neighborhood. I have found a place. It's so close to work. I have grown attached to this job and the opportunity you've given me. I imagine myself at work even when I'm not here. But because of my situation, you know because I'm new to the country, the landlord would like to have a reference from my employer to guarantee that I have a job."

Lise sits back and eyes me carefully. For a while, she says nothing and I listen to the droning ventilation of the central heating system as a lump builds in my throat. "And what do I get if I do this for you?" she asks finally.

Ya rabi. I gulp audibly, suddenly afraid I've overstepped another invisible trip wire somewhere within the culture. "I am happy to do whatever you ask, Ms. Carbonneau."

"Tell you what, Muna. I'll give you your reference on the condition that you accept my offer to become my assistant manager."

"You want to promote me?"

"I do," Lise says matter-of-factly. "I want to offer you more responsibility, along with slightly better pay and, most importantly, stock options. In the six months you've been here, you've sold more plans than any other sales rep, and you have the highest percentage of satisfaction among long-term clients not just at this office, but in all of Québec. Your numbers are so strong in the last quarter that they've even caught the attention of the people from the Toronto head office who were just here."

As I listen to Lise Carbonneau, of all people, numbering off my accomplishments, I can feel my eyes glistening as my face grows hot with eagerness. "I'm so flattered," I finally say. "It would be an honor to be your assistant manager."

"We're going to be a team, working together. You'll take over the orientations of incoming sales reps to start and then manage those that you train moving forward. Business is growing fast, and the head office wants us to expand our space in the coming year. I'm going to need all the best people we have to take Nutri-Fort to the next level. It's going to take a lot of work. I want you to be part of that."

"You can count on me, Ms. Carbonneau."

"Call me Lise, Muna."

"Of course, Lise."

"Feel free to give them my direct extension."

For a moment I look at her curiously and then I remember. "Of course, the reference. I'll do that."

I get up to leave before she decides to change her mind.

"Oh, and Muna," she calls out. I turn around at the door. "There's a private office opening up that you can have. We're moving out some of our payroll to the Toronto office. It'll free you up to make as many calls as you need to, without having to worry about distractions. And for the meetings you'll be having. Andrée at reception will arrange everything for you."

"I'll follow up with her," I say, backing out of her office with a slight bow.

Then I practically skip back to my desk.

Smallah, Muna, Assistant Manager!

I sit down and try to imagine the business cards I'll have made. I can tell that my excitement is obvious because Stéfanie is looking over at me from her desk with a smile.

"Good meeting?" she asks.

"Yes," I nod. "It was a good meeting."

"Good for you," she says, returning to her work.

Mabrouk, Mona, I think to myself. *You did this, not me. And now it's time for you to get back to work.* I look at the call list, prepare the papers she'll need in front of her, pick up the receiver, and dial the number.

"Oui, allô? C'est Mona de Nutri-Fort. How are you today?"

Wallah, the temperature has suddenly jumped ten degrees in one week.

Everything and everyone in Montreal is ready for this change. It's true what Stéfanie and Esther keep saying, I decide one morning while walking to the metro. This must be the most beautiful time of year. Stéfanie says that summer will either be hot and humid or cloudy and windy. Esther says September always feels like there's too much to do. I've already lived through the arrival of winter. I can't see how any other season can replicate the unclenching I feel now.

Bare branches around me are beginning to bud. The last holdouts of snow are disappearing from the streets, except for maybe in back alleyways that receive no light, where little gray mounds of resistance remain. The war is over.

These last few weeks, as I've been watching the snow melt for good, I've learned that winter leaves layers in the snow. Each storm or snowfall lands differently, wet or dry or dense or loose, and buries with it a layer of dust. And once it begins to melt away, that's what you see, the blackest of its memories being revealed again like a series of bad dreams remembered in reverse, losing their sense before they'll be washed away forever with the first spring rain. Yaneh, I feel that way about this past year. Once we move to the new apartment, I want to wash all this away like it never happened. It's official: I'll be moving a month early, on the first of June.

I arrive at the office twenty minutes early and close my new office door behind me. I've yet to bring anything personal into this office to make it mine, so the room has only a white desk, with a chair on either side, and a basic shelving unit upon which I've stacked my client binders. I sit down behind my new desk and stare out the floor-to-ceiling windows, which overlook downtown Montreal. If I look down, I can see the street below, populated with cars the size of the paper clips on my desk.

So far, I've been keeping the blinds of the window looking into the office up so I don't feel too claustrophobic in here. That way I'm still connected to the hotline consultants who work out there at rows of small desks. I was sitting out there just one week ago. Sitting in here, I see the office differently. I'll lower the blinds to make my calls. It's a trick I've learned from watching Lise.

My coworkers congratulated me when Lise first made the announcement, but now I feel a new distance between us. In the kitchen or by the elevators, they no longer seem as relaxed when I'm around. They're more formal when they address me. Tayeb, I've been here longer now than almost all of them, so maybe it's natural for them to look up to me. One or two have even come to my office when Lise is unavailable to ask for help or advice. I encourage such visits.

I keep a bowl of sweets at the corner of my desk and offer them to anyone who thinks to ask me anything.

Today is my first initiation session for new employees. This time, I'm giving the presentation on the company philosophy, guiding them through some of the situations they should expect to encounter, and detailing the pay structure. I'm not nervous; talking in front of people is what teachers do. One by one, I double-check all my slides and slot them into the office slide projector. I raise each one and hold it to the light, making sure they are in the right order and direction. I carry the slide projector into the conference room, toggle with it on the tabletop so its projection meets the screen, and then fill my water glass. A few minutes later, the new employees, all women, file in and take their seats.

"Good morning!" I begin brightly. "My name is Muna Heddad, and I'm assistant manager here at Nutri-Fort's downtown Montreal office. But everyone here calls me Mona. Congratulations on joining the team. I hope you'll be with us for a long time yet. Today we'll be going through an introduction of all the products and services we have to offer, as well as your role in communicating with clients and building your client base. Everyone ready?"

When no one says anything, I begin talking about the company's philosophy on weight gain, how the food packets are designed to take the guesswork out of daily calorie regiments so clients can address the mathematical component of obesity. I cover the company's regional advertising campaign strategy in print and on television, the process through which new clients are assigned to sales reps, how to organize calls, optimal conversation lengths, client log sheets, and the art of filing progress reports. "Sales numbers, phone logs and progress reports will determine how well you are doing," I stress, "so keep yourself well organized. Those among you who can do all that will see their efforts rewarded through the generous commission structure."

"Any questions?" I ask at the end. "If that's all, my door is always open to you anytime you have a client with particular needs."

I go to the kitchen to take a Perrier from the fridge, then return to my office and close the door to indicate I don't want to be bothered while I collect my thoughts after my first presentation. Tayeb, I wonder how many of them won't show up tomorrow, or will leave after they receive their first check.

I am now on a salary, which means that I have benefits and I don't have to line up on Friday afternoons to be handed an envelope with a one-sentence performance review from Lise anymore. Now it's my job to hand out the checks and reviews! Lise and I have even gone out for a lunch in one of the many food courts in the underground city to discuss sales performances. She confided in me the company's plans to restructure for more growth. I'm beginning to think she sees me as a partner now. The whole weight-loss industry has piqued the curiosity of the nationally syndicated daytime talk shows, she said, which is helping spread the word. Now is the time to capitalize and expand. When she was particularly excited, Lise pushed aside her chicken Caesar salad and took my hand so I could feel the electricity of her convictions. Yaneh, I know she's dramatic, but I still blush. "People have been silent on these issues for too long, Mona," she said, letting go. "Imagine a world where everyone got the chance to count calories and talk openly about weight loss."

Yesterday, she even said to me, "Your clothes are looking so much better these days, Mona." As if we're girlfriends and not coworkers. "Can I call you Mona?"

Of course, ma chérie. I smiled.

Staring out across downtown Montreal with a refreshing Perrier in hand, I wonder if Lise and I could one day be friends, go shopping together or walk the mountain or try a restaurant in Chinatown. As Mona, it seems possible.

The days are getting longer. After work, I walk home in the warm sun and watch the university students gathering in crowds on the McGill campus lawn. After the endless winter that pushed everyone indoors, I've forgotten how many people the university brings into the downtown every day. Throughout my neighborhood, from rue Sherbrooke all the way up to avenue des Pins, students have clogged the streets with their moving vans, returning home at the end of the winter semester or flying off to travel the world. I overhear their conversations as they yell to each other across the street from the stoops outside their walk-ups.

I enter our building lobby and say hello to Mr. Saltzman, who I'm genuinely going to miss when we move. I take the elevator upstairs, and when I unlock the door to our apartment, I breathe a small sigh of relief as always when my eyes land on Omar on the couch, watching TV. MusiquePlus is on. I recognize Madonna's voice and begin to dance in front of the TV as I shake off the workday, until the little apricot complains that I'm embarrassing him – in front of who, smallah? I go into his bedroom to change out of my work clothes. In the bathroom, I wipe off the makeup from around my eyes and along my cheeks. I look in the mirror to confirm my work: there, Mona is gone and Muna is back.

The phone rings. I walk back into the living room, ask Omar to turn down the TV, and pick up the receiver.

"Allô?"

"Aiwa, may I speak with Ms. Muna Heddad?" says a gruff, unfamiliar voice.

"Speaking."

"Marhaba, Muna. You don't know me, but I've been looking for you."

"Yes?"

"I'm visiting Canada for a few days. Some people back home asked me to get in touch with you."

"Who?"

"The Khourys."

"Is it about …" I stop myself before saying Halim's name aloud in front of Omar. "Is there news?"

"Yaneh, a body has been located, yes."

My hand shoots up to my mouth. I've been dreading this moment. For years I've waited. "Where?"

"Yaneh, Ms. Heddad, that's what I'm here in Montreal to tell you. Let's meet, and I can share more details with you in person."

Ya rabi, do you think I'll be able to get any sleep tonight? I curl up here in the dip of my sofa bed, and it feels like I'm back in that cellar, the lowest point in my life, cowering all over again in a storage cage. All the effort I've put into building myself up is breaking apart; it's come sliding down like one of those Beirut buildings struck by so many missiles. Halim is everywhere again; he's no longer a secret I keep. I wonder where he's been, what he's thought, how much pain he felt and for how long. Ya Allah, after my memory of him ends, he was forced to live a life that I know nothing about, and eventually it killed him.

At some point, I must have fallen asleep because when I open my eyes the sky outside is beginning to lighten, and I can hear the birds chirping. The nights are starting to warm, and I'm sweating. I can see I'm not alone. Halim sits at the kitchen table, watching the TV's test pattern in the dark. His old undershirt is wrapped tightly around his face, and the TV screen casts blue light across the contour of his eyes, nose, and chin. He looks different than the last few times I've seen him. Long, neglected black curls have clumped in tufts to his balding scalp. He's coated in white dust.

"I'll make us some coffee," I say. I get out of bed and go to the kitchen. Knowing he's sitting there behind me, I can feel the radiation of his accumulated pain, as if he's focusing all his energy on blaming me. "Ya rabi, you must be hungry too," I continue. "Let me put something to eat on the table. The food here, you'll see, isn't like our food. But you get used to it. When was the last time you ate?"

He shrugs.

"You seem upset, ya albeh," I say nervously, trying to make it sound like a joke. "You're not talking much."

Turning around, I untie the shirt from his face, and I inspect the indents of old wounds across Halim's brow. They must have always been there. How could I not see them?

"Yaneh, it's okay. If you want, I can talk enough for both of us."

I lay a little plate of yogurt, olives, and pita bread on the table and then sit down.

"I failed you. I know. I feel it strongly, all the time."

Instinctively, I reach across the table and touch his cold hand. The coffee percolates.

"I know they're going to tell me how you died. I've known for years that one day I would have to hear this news. Still, it's very sudden. It's overwhelming and even violent. I'm different now. It's been hard getting over you."

We sit in silence. I watch him slowly lift food to his mouth, only to put it down again, not ready.

"Will you let me do one thing?" I ask, wanting to help him the only way I can see how. "Can I cut your hair? I'll be gentle. I promise."

With a thick pair of scissors suddenly in hand, I stand over him and pull at the knotted clumps of hair that have formed around the back of his head.

"Can I cut this?" I ask, almost whispering.

I cut the tuft off and look at the tangle of crusted black hairs in my hand, the coiled whites in between them betray his aging, like dust in the snow. When I'm this close, I can feel his breathing on my forearms, see his heartbeat in his neck. I allow my fingers to dance around a swelling of scar tissue interrupting his shoulder. I touch a missing earlobe. I kiss a crease across an upper arm.

"Don't be afraid," I say.

He looks straight ahead. I continue to clip away, growing more obsessed with making the clear, presentable shape of the Halim I remember. But his hair is endless. I keep clipping until there's nothing of him but coarse trimmings on the kitchen floor.

I wake up to Omar shaking my shoulder.

"Wake up, Mama," he says. "You're shaking. You're dreaming."

It takes me a moment to realize where I am. Once I do, I feel both saddened and relieved. I get up, scramble some eggs for Omar's breakfast, and quickly take a shower. I get dressed. I call the office and make arrangements to come in late.

It's raining this morning. After I drop Omar off at school, I catch the avenue du Parc bus toward Outremont. As I stand in a crowd of passengers, holding the overhead strap, I look out at Mount Royal under dark and murky clouds. I ring the bell and push my way off the back of the bus. With my umbrella shielding me, I walk up chemin de la Côte-Sainte-Catherine. As the street bends, I spot something I haven't seen since arriving in Canada. Up the street, on a lawn, up a flagpole, hangs a Lebanese flag. I can make out its red bars, white middle, and green splash where its cedar tree grows. The two-story brown brick building behind it has a plaque out front indicating that it is the Lebanese Consulate. Inside, there's a reception desk facing the door, where I give my name. I'm asked to wait in a warmly lit area that has been decorated to match the opulent living rooms of Beirut, beveled wood, gold trim, glass tabletops and Persian carpets.

Finally, a man in a gray suit comes down the stairs. He says a few words to the woman at the reception desk, then turns around and blows his nose loudly into a handkerchief, which he pushes into his breast pocket. He walks over to me with this same hand extended, his nostrils still flush.

"Ms. Heddad, I am Michel Boutros. We spoke on the phone yesterday. Thank you for coming."

"When you mentioned Halim and the Khourys, how could I not?" I shake his hand. "Do you work for the government?"

"Not really, I'm a lawyer," he says. "Yaneh, I just use this office for business when I pass through Montreal. Let's go upstairs where we can speak more privately."

I follow him back up the stairs to a large office. "Please sit," he points toward a chair facing his desk. "We have a lot to discuss."

"I was surprised by your call yesterday. It's a shock, really."

He frowns. "I'm sorry for your loss. The Khoury family wants me to pass along the news that Halim Khoury, your husband, is now officially deceased."

"I know," I hear myself say, as if I'm watching the conversation from outside. I've lost too much sleep, and now I feel a little delirious. "I mean, I've felt it for a long while. It was only a matter of time before someone made it official. How do you know the Khourys?"

"I have business dealings with Halim's father and brothers. They tell me he was expected to immigrate here with you and your son. He was the one who filed for immigration."

"It was Halim's idea, yes. But in March of 1984, he was kidnapped. That was the last time I ever saw him. A few months later, his family received word that he was as good as dead. They actually said, 'You'll never see him again.' There was never a body to bury. Yaneh, I've been a widow in waiting ever since."

"It's horrible what this war has done to people," Mr. Boutros says.

"Tell me, when did he die?"

He sits back and swivels away from me. "How do I say this? Okay. From the information we've now received, it looks like your husband was alive longer than was assumed."

"What do you mean?"

"The information I have says his body was found by the International Red Cross when they were working in Serghaya, a Syrian village close to the Lebanese border, during activities that took place on November twenty-six of last year."

"And they're sure it's Halim?"

"He still had identification papers, for one. Also, some of the other people there knew him and confirmed his identity to doctors."

"He was in Syria this whole time?"

Mr. Boutros tenses for a moment, then sneezes into his palms. "I'm sorry, it's this damp weather," he says. "It turns out he was in Syria for only several months before he died. The International Red Cross, they found him with a group of forty-six other prisoners who were locked in a warehouse, part of a compound that was raided."

"So he was alive then? I'm sorry, I don't understand."

"The IRC report says only thirteen of the prisoners there were alive at that point and the rest were already dead. Halim, unfortunately, was among the dead. I'm sorry for the nature of these details."

"No, go on. I want to know. How did he die?"

"It looks like a long-term combination of injuries, infections, and malnutrition was most likely a significant factor in his death. Many of the others in the warehouse died that way too. His captors had left them in that room to die, you see."

"Do you know when Halim died?"

"Given the state of his body, he died as little as three days to as long as a week before they were found."

"He made it to last November? That means he almost made it. He lived two and a half years and then died right before he was found," I say, thinking back to what I was doing in November. I see the first snow on Mount Royal, the lookout over the city. Why have I gone back to that moment? It was the first time Halim's voice spoke to me. "What was he even doing there?"

"From what we know, we are fairly certain that, up until August of last year, he was in still in Lebanon, in a bunker in the Beqaa Valley. The family would receive ransom demands from the people who had him. They would always pay. In that situation, he was allowed to work as a mechanic, and he could move freely inside the compound. Another prisoner said each of them had a mattress and his own room with a window. But then, for reasons we don't know, he was traded to a group on the Syrian side of the border. It's the darkest side of these kinds of wars, Ms. Heddad, this trafficking of prisoners among these groups. Prisoners have a value as a kind of money between militias, as bargaining chips in larger negotiations, for ransom also. Halim was traded with four other men. Two of them survived until the raid, and were later cared for by the International Red Cross. They say once they were traded, new ransoms were demanded by their new captors. Those whose families refused to pay ended up in that room."

I'm stunned. "His family was in communication with his captors all these years? They knew where he was?"

"Yaneh, I suppose that's what it means, yes. But they couldn't do anything. Most of the time, Ms. Heddad, you pay the ransom and all you get in exchange is a dead body. There's only so much a family can pay without proof he's still alive."

"This way they get a body and save," I said. "Why did no one try to contact me? I'm his wife. How long have they known he was dead?"

"Maybe since early February."

"It's May now. Yaneh, I don't understand why no one has contacted me this whole time."

"I'm sorry to hear this, Ms. Heddad. I have no information about the family's reasons or motivations on that aspect of this file. I'm just the legal messenger. I can share with you that I'm here now on their behalf. They want this to end for you, as it is has for them."

"But no one from his family thought to call me." I say this quietly, but inside I'm exploding like a car bomb. "Where is the body now?"

"According to my information, a funeral was held. Halim Khoury's body has been laid to rest in his family's plot."

"I can't believe his family would be this cruel," I confess. "All this time I've been waiting and grieving and looking for some kind of answer, they've been burying him and writing us out of their lives. I've been waiting for someone to tell me what happened to him, where he's been this whole time."

"Maybe they thought it was better for you to leave it all behind, as you were already doing."

"It's not for them to decide what I should do or how I should think." But as I say this, I can once again feel the envelope of cash my brother-in-law pressed into my thigh at the Christmas party. Of course they want to decide what I should do and think. "Ya rabi, he died after we moved here. They tricked me into leaving him behind."

I can see it playing out before my eyes now: they pushed my immigration through all that bureaucracy, they gave me money to leave and made sure I left as quickly as possible, and then no one told me about his death, a private family funeral. They killed him, ya Allah, to save their precious ransom.

Mr. Boutros slides a box of Kleenex across the desk. "It's barbaric, Ms. Heddad, what this war has done to people."

"People are barbaric," I say, looking down at my own lap, "and we spend most of our time pretending otherwise."

Mr. Boutros looks at me curiously, as if he doesn't quite understand. "Whatever the case may be, the Khoury family learned I was coming to Montreal and wanted me to contact you on their behalf. They have some of Halim's belongings to offer you. Though I arrived here two weeks ago, it took us some time to track down your telephone number."

"I'm getting ready to move."

"I was lucky to locate you when I did, then." Mr. Boutros presents me with a small box that he places between us. "They want you to have these things."

I look at the box on the desk. That's all that's left of a life, I think, as I look for deeper meaning along the box's beige exterior and layers of clear packing tape. A secret within a secret within a secret.

"I hope you'll accept this as a charitable end to your questions," Mr. Boutros says. "You can grieve now and move on."

By the time I leave the consulate, it's no longer raining but gusting. With my closed umbrella in one hand and the box in a plastic bag flapping in the wind in the other, I walk back down chemin de la Côte-Sainte-Catherine, where I wait for a bus that will take me downtown. Montreal's morning rush is largely over now. When it shows up, I'm able to take a seat. I sit and watch the mountain from the other direction as my damp skin warms. Halim's box – tayeb, some part of Halim – is on my lap. I'm afraid to touch it. All I can think about is what's inside.

It's all so frustrating, the way this situation has been presented to me by the Khourys. Is there anything more sacrilegious than holding a funeral for a man before even telling his wife he's dead? I feel so utterly stupid for not knowing I was being manipulated this whole time. All these years, they'd known he was still alive. They knew he was hidden away in the Beqaa Valley, a pawn in a negotiation they could not win. *They treated you like a child, Muna,* I can hear Mona say. *I was a child when they knew me,* I reply. I don't think I grew up till I moved here. I still hate myself for letting them cast me aside.

I'm trying hard to remember the Halim I knew before this whole ordeal began and before his family sought to control me. But from half a world away, I'm finding it hard to see that far back with much clarity. The man who's visited me all those nights is fading away. There must have been a time when nothing stood between our love, I think to myself, almost asking. Or am I just holding on to a moment up above the clouds in Kfar Mechki when we were still too young to know any better, before his engagement, his family, the war, the immigration? *You couldn't have been that far apart, Muna*, I hear Mona say. *He was my stranglehold*, I say. *Sometimes he was your embrace*, she replies.

I stand up to ring the bell. The bus drops me off, and I walk along De Maisonneuve Boulevard. I decide that, no matter what is in that box, I did love a Halim all this time, and that's no different whether it was real or imagined. Right? And maybe I'm better off because I believed in that love as much as I did. It's the lie that got me through, not the truth. It's the lie that entwines around me like a vine, not the other person. I want to keep that lie alive. I step into the elevator of the office building and press the wrong floor by mistake, not sure what I believe about anything anymore.

When I finally walk through the Nutri-Fort office, I don't say hello to any of my new hotline operators who edge toward me for help but then decide against it when they catch sight of the dark cloud I've brought in with me. I enter my office and close the door. I sit down and gaze out the floor-to-ceiling window for a long time. I study the docks and train yards beyond, the river, the South Shore.

This is my new home, I think. This is where I feel most myself now. I didn't think so before, but now I do. This is what I've realized most clearly this morning, why I'm afraid of what I have to do next and where it will take me.

I place the box on the corner of my desk, the plastic bag's handles still straining up like an overeager student. Quietly distraught, I peel away the plastic bag. In my desk drawer, I find an X-Acto knife and draw its blade. With all the morning's mixed emotions, I stab the top of the box and slice through its taped flaps. I'm like a Khoury: I locate the fault line running between two parts and exploit its gaps to get what I want. Even though I don't need to, I stab the box again, and then a third time. I think it will feel good, but I only feel worse. I drop the X-Acto knife and fall back into my chair, mentally and even physically exhausted. The smell from the box's seal opening, however faint, intoxicates me. It smells like another world. I lean over and pull open the two divided flaps, letting out its earthiness and antiquity as I peel back the last remaining tethers of tape.

Inside, there's old Arabic newspaper bunched around another plastic bag, which I pull out and untie. The first thing I pull out is Halim's old wallet. I recognize its look and feel immediately. As I hold it in my hand, I can see it clearly on the little table by the apartment door or resting on the kitchen counter. I've seen it so many times before and never once gave it a second thought. But now all those times flood back in one sudden flash. I open it up and find his identification card inside. There are a few other papers in there. I hold it up to my nose and breathe it in, wanting to know where it's been this whole time.

The second item in the box is a jar full of sand. I set it down on my desk. It's as tall as my Rolodex. The lid is rusted. The sand inside is rough and clumpy, not desert sand but maybe the sandy dirt from the foot of a mountain range where nothing grows, like in Syria. I look at its sides and bottom and see only the same sand from every angle.

I sit back and wonder what a jar of sand is supposed to mean to me. I lock onto this question for who knows how long, until the phone rings and abruptly snaps me back to reality. By the second ring, I've blown my nose and wiped the edges of my eyes. By the third, I pick up. "Nutri-Fort, Muna speaking … Oui, bonjour, Suzanne … No, it's no bother … Yes, you can tell the client that we have several introductory packages that make it simpler than ever to get started."

It's one of the more recent hires, only her second week on the phones. My trance finally evaporates. I put the wallet and the jar back where they came from and give my attention to these responsibilities that require me to be in the present moment. I can't spend the whole day trying to decipher a puzzle from the past. After lunch, I have a meeting with my sales staff. I take them through the weekly numbers and preview the details of Nutri-Fort's upcoming Summer Swimsuit Challenge campaign. I let my work carry me away like the current of a fast-moving river. I let Mona take charge, while the part of me that's flailing quietly drowns inside.

Along the way, coworkers cough and sniffle and blow their noses, blink their red-rimmed eyes, muffle their words through swollen sinuses. Suddenly everyone around me in the city is sick! One of the ladies in the break room calls it "a spring cold." When the weather suddenly warms and Montreal switches to summer, the immune system is so unprepared that everyone gets congested and achy. It begins with children coming home from school, their sleeves thick with mucus streaks. Then boxes of Kleenex pop up on every desk. Employees pass around bottles of Advil and Tylenol and cough drops. The number of empty desks spreads, and we end up with a lot of turnover among the hotline operators, who use the days off to find other jobs.

When I get back to my apartment, I leave the box on the shoe rack by the door, confident it won't be noticed. There are now open boxes everywhere. I'm packing up everything we've accumulated over the past ten months. Instead of kissing Omar on the head when I come in, I undress by the ironing board and sneak naked across the hall with a fresh towel in hand. Under a steady stream of hot water I decide I will not tell Omar any of this. Making an executive decision as I would at work, I decree that he must never know anything more than what he thinks he knows about the circumstances of his father's death. Tayeb, I don't see why this new truth has to replace the truth he currently lives with. Who's to say today's truth isn't just another unwelcome story invented by the Khourys in their never-ending attempts to ruin my life? Today's truth only confirms that I've lied to him. Once Omar realizes that, he will see everything I've done for him as a deceit and not protection. And I will lose him, the one person I can never afford to lose.

After my shower, I prepare dinner while watching TV out of the corner of my eye. We eat on the couch today, to distract from my shattered state. Predictably we say nothing, Omar lost to the mindless motions of another family comedy. His TV friends have a father and a mother and brothers and sisters and a dog. They laugh and hug and care for each other, and when they sit down for dinner at their loud, generous table, I'll bet anything he'd rather be having dinner with them. So I let him do that tonight.

My head feels hot to the touch. My mind feels like it's burning up with bad ideas. Am I taking things too far because of this anger inside me? After I hustle Omar into brushing his teeth and force him to bed early – "Ya albeh, we have a very busy weekend coming up!" – I pop a thermometer in my mouth and suck on it like a cigarette. I read its mercury carefully against the lamplight. I have a fever. With that confirmation, I let myself feel weak. I take two Tylenol. I make myself a tea. For several hours, I sit in front of the TV and say nothing. My thoughts are all uncomfortable, writhing and restless. Exhausted yet unable to sleep, I feel the fever thickening. I don't feel well at all.

I pull out the box from this morning's meeting, place it on the coffee table, and take out the jar of sand and the wallet. I pick up the wallet and look at it closely. This is what he had with him when he died. Or maybe it was sent to the Khourys at some point to convince them to pay a ransom. One by one, I push open and finger through its slots and pockets. His identification card is here, as well as a few business cards for car dealers and other mechanics.

Is this even Halim's wallet? Yaneh, I should recognize it more forcefully, I say to myself. Earlier I thought I did, but now that my temperature's up and my senses heightened, I'm not so sure. I empty out its cards and line them up on the table. With nothing in it, the wallet's leather is thin and stretched. I feel its skin with my fingers to see if I can locate what it's hiding from me. I'm so hot I feel electric. I am a hotline, I think, a conduit to all the answers I crave. Something in the stitching of this material must have remained pure and unmanipulated enough to offer me an unassailable truth. I press my trembling fingers deeper into its creases, and that's when I feel the tiny bump that shouldn't be there.

At the very bottom of a pocket, I feel a fold. I dig down inside, so thoroughly I almost push my whole head into the wallet, and back there in its very farthest corner I touch a lump of paper with the tip of my nail. It's so small I have a hard time ferreting it out. In the dark, I have to dig in there with the handle end of a teaspoon to finally dislodge it. It bounces across the coffee table and lands on the carpet. I feel the carpet's thick pile for it, find it, and set it back down in front of me. There. It tried to get away but it couldn't. A flaw in the Khoury plan. Delicately, I unfold the little piece of paper that feels as though it could disintegrate at any moment. By the time I lay it flat against the tabletop, I can make out fading Arabic script on it. I hold it to the light and see numbers. There's a dash that makes me think it's a Lebanese phone number.

I set down the wallet and begin to rethink the jar of sand. Ya Allah, my mind races with possibilities, so fast I might pass out. It occurs to me again that there may be something inside. From under the sink, I get out the mop bucket and set it on the kitchen table. The lid on the jar is too tight, so I use the tip of a spoon to work my way under its seal and break its grip. The rusty lid fights me with its claws, and as my fingers slip with sweat I almost scream in frustration. But then it finally comes loose. Grains of sand fall from its grooves as I unscrew it the rest of the way off. Is this Syrian sand, I wonder again, collected from the scorched earth where he wasted away? Or did a Khoury scoop this up from a vacant lot behind their apartment complex? I pour the sand from the jar into the bucket. Something else falls in along with the sand. I dig it out: a small wooden carving of a horse, the kind Halim used to make with a carving knife for Omar during those long nights in the cellar.

After a day of clenching, my heart softens. Looking at that small horse in my palm, I am reminded that even though the world is built on transactions of uncaring and gestures of exclusion, there is still kindness that hides in its folds and between its layers, just waiting to be revealed. This horse is that truth I needed, pure and unmanipulated. No Khoury could have guessed this. Halim was thinking of us. He yearned to be with us. I squeeze the horse in my clammy fist, wanting to absorb all the thought and energy that went into making it. My head hurts. I can feel grains of sand caught in my eyelids.

Setting the horse carvings side by side on the kitchen table, united at last, I begin to feel more hopeful. I'm reaffirmed. For much of today, I lost faith in my love and in myself. My desires felt selfish, self-serving. I began imagining things that aren't there. But now I've been vindicated. Despite this fever, or maybe because of it, I can see clearly now. I was right to feel love. I was correct to let it comfort me. I feel a chill, a shudder. My teeth chatter. I hold myself in place, unable to move. I feel so weak. I have only enough energy left to turn one thought over and over again, as I gaze at those two horses together.

I do not know if it's dream or reality when I pick up the receiver, dial the international code, Lebanon's country code, and then the numbers on the small piece of paper. It might not even be a phone number, but after the horse, I have to know. International calls are like gambling: yaneh, you never know the outcome, but either way it's expensive. Maybe you get hold of an operator, occasionally the line connects directly, but mostly numbers to the other end of the world just disappear into space. I hear a delay in my dialing, and I'm not sure if it's my head or the line. The line crackles. A long dial tone breaks through, almost against its will, the sign of a temperamental connection. It beeps once and then pauses. It beeps a second time, exhausted. Three times, then four. On the fifth ring, I hear someone pick up on the other end and breathe.

It's so dark at this time of night and my temples pulsate with such force that I'm not sure where I am or who I'm calling. "Halim, is that you?" I let out.

There's a pause, a thundercloud of static. "No, madame," a man says back.

"Do you know who I'm talking about," I say, the receiver sweating in my hands. "Do you know Halim?"

"Halim who?"

"Halim Khoury."

There's a long pause, and for a moment I fear that I'm talking to myself, that no one is actually there. But then he says, "Yes, I do. Who is this?"

"I'm his wife."

"Muna," the man says. "Is that right? He talked about you."

"How do you know my name? Who are you?"

"My name is Elias. For two years, Halim and I slept in the same room. We had lots of time to talk. Before Syria, we got to know each other well. How did you find me?"

"This number was in his wallet."

"That's right," he says. "I remember when I gave it to him. This is the phone line at my father's factory, where I worked before I was kidnapped. I gave him this number to contact me if he ever made it out alive."

"They say he died."

"I know. He died beside me."

"Did he suffer?"

"For a long time we didn't. But then we were moved, and we did."

"And you lived."

"It's so arbitrary."

Through tears, I whisper, "I'm happy he was able to find peace."

"Truthfully, ya binteh, most days I wish I died there. That way I wouldn't have to remember it. He always talked about you and his son. He loved you very much. He talked about Canada and how you'd move there."

"We did," I say. "That's where I'm calling you from. We've been here almost a year."

"Good," Elias says. "Then his wish came true. All he ever said was that he hoped you would go on with your life. That you wouldn't wait. He always said, there's no point in waiting. No one has any idea what's in store."

"Inshallah, ya Elias."

"Inshallah, ya Muna," he says back.

He starts saying something else, but his voice gets lost in static. The line crackles loudly, and then it goes dead. When I try calling back, the connection is no longer there. I fall asleep, and when I next come to, it's light out.

Yaneh, was it real? Did it happen? In the end, I can't tell. I called the number again several times after I first got cut off, and was met with only a dial tone. The number led nowhere or could no longer connect. I tried it again the next day, and I was lucky enough to catch a busy signal. The time I tried after that, I was back to a dead line. But I remember every word of our conversation so clearly, and it impacted me so deeply, that I can't simply discount it. Maybe the fever created what I needed to hear. My temperature only begins to come down by the middle of the next day. In the end, I'm taking my first-ever sick day. I let Omar walk to school by himself in the morning. I didn't want to, but that list of things I told myself I'd never allow and then done? Yaneh it's getting pretty long.

I lie in the sofa bed, my nose stuffy, relieved that I don't have to talk to anyone. Tomorrow is Saturday. I've moved the French lessons to Sunday this week, because our new beds will be delivered to the new apartment, and after that we'll spend the day walking our boxes over. We don't have that much to move. Our clothes, some bed linens that I'll happily replace after we've settled in, an ironing board, a mop and bucket, a box of cleaning products for the kitchen and bathroom, papers we've collected, the VCR. That is all we have after ten months. I'm lying in what feels like an ending. After this is over, I will no longer have this sofa bed with its dip, but it will still know all my secrets, and maybe it will reveal them to the next person who sleeps in it.

Tayeb, I decide, after we move this weekend, from that point on I don't see any reason not to be Mona. Who in Montreal, where everyone is so preoccupied with individual pursuits, is going to notice that I've substituted one little letter?

When our immigration hearing comes up, I'll make it permanent. A name is a connection to a place and a world, but that world and that place are making things harder for me. It can be so tiring having to be two people at once! I want to spend more time with the version of me that bought a bedroom set last weekend. I am inclined to permanently employ the version of me who will guide Brault & Martineau movers up the stairs and into my new bedroom, where they can set down my new queen-sized bed, my new dresser, and my new vanity, but only after I say where. I yearn to be the me who rips the plastic covering from new furniture to smell its newness: never used, never touched. I am not interested in opening any more old boxes filled with memories that make no sense. I will not stare at a jar of sand or wonder where along the way everything went wrong.

En tout cas, I'm not so sure the world is as uncaring as I sometimes accuse it of being. There have been moments when, if I'm searching for guidance and I'm desperate enough for an answer, the fabric of circumstance will reach out to me and offer me a signal, subtle and imperceptible to everyone but me, a gift, and if I am of a mindset to listen to it, to not question its possibility, I can find some peace in what it has to say by connecting lines between the past and present. My time in this apartment has taught me this much: if I put signals out into the world, I will get signals back. I can never prove it, but I can tell you it's true.

When I finally go wash up, I will leave Muna in this mattress for someone else to find, and I'll finish taping up the boxes around the apartment.

There's no point in waiting any longer. I get up, I take off the sweat-soaked clothes I've worn since I first started feeling sick, and instead of throwing them in the laundry basket, I stuff them into an open garbage bag in the corner of the room. I won't be needing them again. I step in the shower, and it feels like a baptism. I stand under the rush of hot water and let it wash away all the doubts I've collected. Yaneh, it's strange but ever since the phone call I truly feel like I am loved. I no longer feel the need to hear Halim's voice comforting me. I no longer regret any of the choices I've made. I no longer think back and lament the past. When I dry myself off, I feel free, hungry. Maybe it's how a person normally feels after a fever has broken.

Omar comes home. He unlocks the door and looks genuinely caught off guard to see me there, at the kitchen table, the two horses staring back at me proudly. He's used to having the apartment empty for the next two hours.

"Hi, ya habibi," I say. "Are you hungry? Can I make you a sandwich?"

"Sure," he says. He picks up the new horse. "Another one? I thought there was only one."

"It turns out there were always two this whole time."

"Baba made these. I remember he used to carve them."

"He did, ya albeh."

"It's nice that there's two. This way they can be together. Where did it come from?"

"I found it while packing, ya habibi."

"Can I keep them in my room in the new apartment? I'd like to have something from Baba."

"Of course you can."

He looks around. "Are we moving today?"

"Tomorrow, when the beds arrive. Today, we can walk over and pick up the key. Maybe take some boxes over."

"I can't wait to sleep in my new room."

"Me too."

Yaneh, it's nice to be excited about the same goal. I would like for us to start again in the new apartment, to fix the bond between us that I've had to sacrifice this year and to make sure I keep him close. At the end of June, the French courses in the church basement will take a break for the summer. After that, I don't know if I'll go back when it can all start up again in September. I want to make sure I have time for Omar so we can have some projects together. But I don't want to decide right now. The summer off will be good for us. Because of my new position, I even get two weeks off, paid, a real summer vacation. For the rest of the time, I'm using some of my savings to put Omar in an affordable day camp at the downtown YMCA. Winnie told me about it, so he'll be there with Chang. I don't want him to sit in an apartment all summer when he could be playing outside.

I take my temperature again just to make sure the fever is really gone. My face is puffy, but beyond that I feel normal again. We sit around and watch TV, aware that it's the last time we'll do that here. I listen to rush hour traffic come and go. The afternoon sun begins to fade.

"Yallah," I say after he finishes a sandwich I've prepared for him. "Let's go get those keys."

We take the elevator downstairs, and I wave hello to Mr. Saltzman. The neighborhood's students completed the last of their exams a few weeks ago, and most of them have left the city. Yaneh, they're lucky. Many of them will never know what it's like to lose everything and start again. They may learn about it in classes and develop opinions on what should be done to make the world a better place, and for many of them that's all they'll ever need to think about. *Good for them*, I think. At least the neighborhood is quieter now that they're gone. Outside, the evening air is fresh and the trees are blossoming and the flowers in the planters are beginning to bloom. At this time of day, the sun begins to dip down toward the mountain, and the buildings cast long shadows across the streets. I ask Omar to hold my hand because we're crossing streets and there are cars, but really it's just because I don't get too many chances to hold his hand anymore, and how much longer will he let me? Hand in hand, we walk down Milton Street, past the pizzeria, past another student restaurant, past The Word bookstore and the dépanneur.

It only takes ten minutes to walk to our new apartment.

I ring the bell for Mike the landlord's apartment, and he comes down to open the door for us. He takes us into our empty new home. I hand him an envelope from my purse, which contains the first and last months' rent in cash I've saved from the French lessons.

He takes the envelope and, without counting the bills, pushes it into his back pocket. "Okey dokey," he says, pointing over to some papers he's left out on the kitchen counter, "once you sign here, here, and here, initial here, and print your name there, it's all yours."

The papers list damages I am responsible for, how much I would owe in the event something happens to the walls, the floors, the cabinetry, the windows. They seem mostly directed at the irresponsible students who previously lived here. I bend over and, yaneh, I think hard before I move ahead with what I want to do. Delicately but fluidly, I sign my name as Mona Heddad. It's a minor change in an identity that no one will ever catch among all the rings and flourishes of my signature. It's mostly for me. But then I have to print it out at the end. There's nowhere to hide, and so out I come as Mona Heddad, on this piece of paper that will probably never be looked at again. I set the pen down, and as Mona I accept the keys. Then Mike leaves and we're in our new apartment all alone. The ceilings are so high I can hear an echo when I walk.

"Can we stay here tonight?" Omar asks.

"Our beds don't arrive until tomorrow," I say.

"I can sleep on the floor. I don't care."

To be honest, I also don't care. "Let's see if we can make beds out of pillows and blankets," I hear myself say.

"We'll have a sleepover!" I can see Omar growing excited.

He runs over to the window in the back, opens the door leading out to the balcony, and looks down at the yard, with its big maple tree providing plenty of shade, and its view of the mountain. When I join him, I see that the sun is going to set right over the mountain's tree line soon. The trees are all bursting green with new leaves. How long will it take, I wonder. I check my watch. Maybe twenty minutes at most. I sit down on the first step of the circular metal staircase to watch it. Yaneh, I never once thought watching a sunset would be something I'd want to do. Who has the courage to expect such moments when they only ever happen in TV movies? But now the bottom arc of the sun is about to touch the top of Mount Royal, and I know it's arbitrary that this will be our view from now on, but it still feels like it's happening especially for me. I know that at least half the other balconies in this neighborhood face this very same way, that there's nothing about this world that's bending to please me in particular. But ya Allah, I still can't wait to see it.

ACKNOWLEDGMENTS

This story was inspired by circumstances that have taken up space in my head for decades. In Muna Heddad, I see something of my mother's story when we first landed in Montreal in the eighties. A French teacher by training, she also couldn't find work in education as a newly arrived immigrant and resorted to working at a weight-loss center, selling boxed food to make ends meet. From today's vantage point, this episode in her life speaks to me in ways that were not evident in childhood.

I would like to thank Karolina Armata-Machnik for always being my first and most honest reader. My long-running collaboration with Simon Dardick, Nancy Marrelli, and Véhicule Press has grown into one of my life's most rewarding and enduring relationships. I feel blessed to have the creative license they've afforded me to develop my own artistic practice and, as Esplanade's editor, to cultivate a diverse network of writers whose books have helped evolve my own fiction. Liz Johnston, as editor for this book, brought sharp insight, a confident scalpel, and much-needed perspective to this story, the effects of which are immeasurable.

DIMITRI NASRALLAH is the author of four novels, including *Hotline*, a Canadian bestseller that was long-listed for the 2022 Giller Prize and was a 2023 finalist for Canada Reads. Nasrallah was born in Lebanon in 1977, during the country's civil war, and moved to Canada in 1988. His previous books include *The Bleeds* (2018); *Niko* (2011), which won the Hugh MacLennan Prize for Fiction; and *Blackbodying* (2005), which won Quebec's McAuslan First Book Prize. His books have also been nominated for the Dublin Literary Award and the Grand Prix du Livre de Montréal. Nasrallah lives in Montreal, where he is the editor of Esplanade Books and teaches creative writing at Concordia University.